Young Men
Shall See

Quantity discounts are available on bulk orders. Contact info@TAGPublishers.com for more information.

TAG Publishing, LLC
2618 S. Lipscomb
Amarillo, TX 79109
www.TAGPublishers.com
Office (806) 373-0114
Fax (806) 373-4004
info@TAGPublishers.com

ISBN: 978-1-934606-37-7

First Edition

Copyright © 2012 Scott Thompson

Young Men Shall See

Kortney &
Chris,
Thank you for
your support.

Scott Thompson
6/20/12

Scott Thompson

To my best friend and wife, Rhonda
Because of you the world is possible

Acknowledgements

I must thank my mother for typing my stories when I was a child. You were the first person to support and believe in me. Thanks to my little boys. You taught me the meaning of life. I have to thank my highly talented brother, Tim, and all my family. I also would like to thank author Gwen Morrison, author Heather Sharfeddin, Major Robert C. Davis, Dr. Leverett Butts PhD, Scott Kennedy, and Jason Tillis. A big thank you goes to Dee Burks and the folks at TAG Publishing. You've gone above and beyond and I truly appreciate everything. Thanks to the love of my life, Rhonda. Every time I look at you, you're more beautiful than the last time.

About the Author

Scott Thompson lives in Georgia with his wife, two boys, and a dog intent on world domination. He has lived in the South his entire life where the interesting, intelligent, and eccentric people have enriched his imagination. He enjoys being outdoors and traveling. Scott holds degrees in history, business administration, and computers.

www.AuthorScottThompson.com

Prologue

I grew up in a place missed by time. In my isolated Southern town, the wind rolled in from the swamps and through the trees and whispered to us that God had chosen this place because it was sinless and pure. My home of River Falls was wrapped in a curve in the Wahoo River, some miles south of Atlanta. It was Southern, but the label meant nothing as I knew nothing else. Sure, there was a place up north where odd sounding and condescending Yankees came from. A few had even dared to move to our Eden, but their foolish ideas hadn't yet contaminated our ideal world, so we felt safe from the sins of the North. Our grandfathers had fought in World War II and our fathers in Vietnam, but other than that most remained in the tranquility of our pines and oaks. Despite the peace, there was a monster coming our way that sprawled slowly from Atlanta. Like a swarm of locust devouring crops, development was seeking out every last tree and every potentially good place to build another neighborhood, another shopping center, another office park. Change was coming, but most people in our faux idyllic town ignored the unstoppable force.

When we became teenagers, boredom grew like a moth in a cocoon fighting to escape, and the peace created by our parents became a prison. We sought excitement and adventure. We sought anything but the sinless, pure, and average of the faux idyllic. There were few thrills for us, so we created them. We had fished the river as children but grew tired of catfish and fish entrails, so we found new hobbies: dreaming of the future, drinking, driving fast, and practicing the art of making love. Maybe the art of making love is an exaggeration as we were happy to even get to first base and our art could only be compared with the crayon drawings of a toddler. With a perspective on life that only consisted of 17 years, the future always seemed so far away where a year felt like a decade and high school an eternity. Yet, despite our eternity, we chose not to waste a moment.

In River Falls, we all knew our caste, just like we knew our religious denomination, even if we hadn't been to church in years, or ever. River Falls was full of privileged kids who took their mother's last name as their first so that no one would ever mistake where they came from as if their mother's name had lasting importance. There were others of this breed that simply invented names so odd and ludicrous that no one would ever copy them, ensuring they would stand out among the common. Names of total gibberish that looked good on a business sign but sounded senseless elsewhere, ensuring that they could never function in any other society but the dying one their great, great grandfathers had built, a society created when negroes, white trash, and the farming community bowed down to Southern aristocracy. As strong as these castes were, there were no laws or rules to enforce them and the unwritten and unsaid rules were starting to be broken. We no longer bowed down to them, but we were often reminded of our place below them, even as the social classes crumbled.

My resentment toward the old aristocracy and their silly names may have tipped you off that I was not among the elite of River Falls, nor was I among the poor, despite the scar of poverty that remained with my parents who had clawed their way from the gutters. I belonged somewhere in the middle. I experienced life in a place that was safe from the vices of the wealthy and safe from the pains of poverty. My place in the middle was sought by many, but it was a place that weighed like a chain of boredom on my soul.

As the 1980s came to a close so did my boyhood. I united with a band of friends who were struggling, as I was, to break the bonds of boredom, childhood, and place. We fought to break the weight of our pasts while trying to protect our idyllic world. We fought ourselves more than we fought others. We fought in the revolution side by side.

Chapter 1

I squirmed as eight hands lifted my body onto the sacrificial altar. A beam of moonlight broke through the trees and illuminated the stone altar that was now my bed. Or maybe it was the light from a flashlight. I couldn't tell through my blindfold. The icy air tasted of old foggy swamp and burned my lungs as my chest shifted up and down quickly like a victim of asthma.

The group of four began to chant, "S.S.D...S.S.D…S.S.D."

"Brothers!" a deep voice yelled. The chanting stopped immediately.

It took me a moment, but then I recognized the voice of Keif, the older brother of my friend Cassady.

The new silence revealed thunder in the distance that echoed slightly off the towering trees. Keif broke the silence, "Brothers, tonight we are gathered to induct a new member into the Society of Social Deviants. There can never be more than four and as I pass into the world of adults, I offer you Gus. In this sacred place we dedicate our alliance to him and him to us. Do the brothers accept?"

"Yes," four voices avowed in unison.

"Augustus Longfellow Ambrose do you accept the S.S.D.?"

"I do, uh, yes," I said with a shaky voice.

"Welcome to the family. You can take off your blindfold and begin your journey."

What did he mean by 'journey,' I wondered as I pulled down the blindfold to find myself four feet from the ground on a stone urn planter. Dark, shadowy trees surrounded the urn and English ivy climbed half way to the top of the makeshift altar. I couldn't see much beyond a few feet into the darkness, but the sound of night creatures hovered around us. The blackness concealed things I didn't dare consider.

"Where am I?" I asked.

"Gethsemane Gardens. We are the protectors of this secret garden," Keif answered.

Gethsemane Gardens had once been an outdoor theater where Southern actors and musicians honed their skills before launching many successful careers. By the 1940s Gethsemane was world renowned, but then the quaint stream that flowed through the center of the garden was flooded, turning most of it into a swamp that drowned gazebos, tea houses and covered many of the stone structures built by workers from the early 1930s. The workers were Masons who had been seeking any work they could find during the Depression.

The Society of Social Deviants had been founded in the 1950s by four brothers whose father had built many of the monuments. When the gardens began to flood and lost their obvious usefulness, people started stealing the stone structures for their homes. To protect their father's legacy, the brothers camped at the gardens nightly waiting for thieves. When the brothers caught a River Falls commissioner pushing a statue of Dionysus strapped to hand trucks, they knocked the man unconscious, stripped the commissioner naked, tied him up, and dropped him off in front of the police department. Of course, they were arrested for false imprisonment, assault, and kidnapping, but the city commissioner was too embarrassed to press charges. This act earned the brothers a reputation and, with that, they started the Society of Social Deviants in order to "protect the legacy and historical sculptures of Gethsemane, and to generally be a nuisance to anyone deserving of punishment as deemed deserving by members of the S.S.D."

Everyone at River Falls High School knew of the S.S.D., but no one knew who they were, although I was sure Keif was a member when I noticed a tattoo with the letters on his ankle the summer before while swimming at his house. Since the founding, there had always been four members, with members being replaced when others graduated or grew too old to cause havoc.

I received my invitation in my locker a week before. The invitation stated:

THE S.S.D. IS WATCHING YOU. IF YOU ARE INTERESTED IN BEING A MEMBER OF THIS EXCLUSIVE SECRET SOCIETY WEAR BLACK ON TUESDAY.
TELL NO ONE

I did as requested and was approached by Keif's little brother, Cassady. "Hey man. What's with the black clothes?"

"Nothing. Just felt like wearing black today."

"Good answer. I'll pick you up tonight."

Cassady once told me that he'd die for me. He was drunk when he said it, but I believed him. Now we were both seniors and had been good friends since junior high school. I considered my friendships with Cassady, Ogie, and Darwin to be the best I had ever known, even though I tried to stay away from Cassady in school, thanks to his uncanny ability to find trouble. I didn't know what it was with him, but boy, he could get into some trouble. In Cassady's first three years of high school, he had been suspended six times and even spent a month in reform school. His parents threatened to send him to military school in Gainesville if he didn't shape up and that motivated him to avoid trouble. Or to at least hide it better at school. I met Cassady at Ogie's house when I was 13. Cassady's father was the groundskeeper for Ogie's parents. The two boys cared little about employer-employee relations and became fast friends. Ogie introduced us and, from that time, we became an unbreakable team.

Now I was a member of the secret society and finally saw the others as my eyes focused without the blindfold. I recognized Ogie's voice in the car after Cassady had picked me up at my house and blindfolded me, but I was surprised to see Darwin. How in the hell did I not know that my best friends were part of the S.S.D.? I felt betrayed and honored at the same time.

"Welcome to the S.S.D. son." A smiling Darwin held out his hand and helped me down from the altar. Then he reached behind his head and pulled a bottle of Jack Daniels whiskey from his beige canvas pack. "You're gonna need some of this. Especially after that. Got the shit scared out of you I'm bettin'?"

"Not too bad," I said. "I didn't know you were in the S.S.D. I didn't know the S.S.D. was real, but—"

He cut me off, "Oh, it's real son. It's as real as a ghost."

"What?" I asked as I took the bottle. I drank enough to appease the crowd and passed the bottle to Ogie. "I didn't know what was going to happen, but now that I'm here I have to say I'm a little pissed that none of you told me you were members."

"I'm outta here. Y'all tell him what he needs to know. Good luck with the S.S.D." Keif shook my hand. "And another thing. You're not a member. This isn't a club. It's part of your soul," he said before turning and walking into the woods.

"So what do I need to know?" I asked.

"The most important thing to keep in mind is secrecy. After that...destruction," Cassady said and then spit into the grass.

"Destruction? What are you talking about?" Ogie asked, almost grunted.

"Well, not random destruction, but destruction to those that deserve it." Cassady laughed before hugging me.

Darwin held his hand up as if to take control of the conversation. "What my two friends are attempting to articulate is that we mostly just have fun, try to get laid, drink more than we should, and occasionally drive too fast. But sometimes, very rarely, we take care of those that need taking care of."

"That's what we already do," I said. "Except for the destruction part. What does that mean?" I asked, fearing I'd joined the mob.

"Don't worry about it. We've never had to take care of anyone since we've been in the S.S.D., but I hope we get to soon," Cassady responded with a smile and his eyes shaped like zeros. "Look Gus, we don't really do much of anything we don't already do with you. We've only been out here a few times before this. I've been in the S.S.D. for about a year and just brought Darwin and Ogie in a couple of months ago. We couldn't bring anyone else in until my brother was ready to leave. There can only be four members at a time and Keif stayed around to teach us the history and to bring us out here a few times until he knew we weren't scared of the dark."

"I'm glad I'm in, but a little upset too that I was the last one invited."

Cassady put his hands on each of my shoulders and squeezed them. "Lighten up buddy. It ain't nothing to worry 'bout. The only thing we really try to do is to get laid, just like always. We try, try, try."

"Tried. I've done it boys," Darwin exclaimed.

"Well you crazy beaver hound. You finally got some," Cassady said before pushing Darwin and almost knocking him to the ground.

"What, did Miescha finally hand over her V card to you?" Ogie asked with his upper class Southern accent.

"Yes, she gave me her virginity, but…"

"But what, son? You've got to spill the beans here," Cassady said with a crooked smile.

Darwin's face twisted and he became serious. "I'll tell y'all about it, but you have to promise not to laugh."

"Why would we laugh? We're not going to laugh. No one gets it right the first time, if that's what you're worried about," I said. "I would be happy to get laid, and to be honest I'm happy I didn't just get laid. You never know what's going to happen when you're tied up and blindfolded. But sorry, go on Darwin."

Darwin took a deep breath, looked at the ground, and then brushed his hand through his black hair. "I really like her. You know we've been sorta dating for months now. Not really dating, but sorta off and on I guess. Anyway, every time we would get close she would push me away and, trying to respect her, I backed off, you know? It was all cool. Whatever she wanted, I figured. Well, last weekend things were right. I could just tell somehow that was going to be the night.

"Now, I'm not going to give you cats all the details, but I'll tell you it was the most amazing experience I've ever had. We made love twice and after the love-making, Miescha started crying." Darwin paused and looked away before continuing.

"I thought I'd really touched her. You know, that we'd just shared a beautiful moment or something. I pulled her close to me to hold her. You know, women like that after making love." Darwin looked back at us and shifted his jaw to the left and then right. "But she pushed away. Then she told me that she'd been thinking that she might be a lesbian and, after having sex with me, she knew for sure. Making love to me confirmed to her that she was a lesbian."

Cassady looked at the ground, turned away from us, and grabbed a tree. His back shook as he giggled like a school kid. I laughed out loud, forgetting my promise.

Ogie hugged Darwin and then said, "After hugging you, I can confirm that I am 100% heterosexual."

"You can all kiss my sweaty ass," Darwin responded.

"What? You mean to tell me your ass is sweating in this weather? Man, you've got big problems," I said.

"Remind me to never tell any of you anything important again," Darwin said and then walked ahead of us down the trail away from the urn. "I share the single best and worst night in my teenage life with y'all and this is the response I get. I'd done better telling my mother than y'all."

"At least you're getting laid," I said as I kicked the dirt. I felt guilty for laughing and tried to repair my jab. "And with lesbians no less. I think that sends you to the next level."

Darwin grabbed Cassady by the arm, smiled, and said, "Now we just have to get Gus and Ogie laid."

Ogie lifted his hand like he was asking a question and said, "Speak for yourselves gentlemen. I am getting laid. Even though I'd prefer not to speak of it so crudely."

"What?" I asked.

"Yeah, What? Tell us more, son," Cassady asked.

"Maybe later. Do me a favor and don't tell anyone, okay."

"Sure. We're the S.S.D. You don't even need to ask. But in the feeling of professional confidentiality, I must request that you tell us who she is. I'm not sure the bylaws of the Society allow you to keep such juicy secrets," Darwin stated.

"What bylaws?" Cassady said with a laugh.

Ogie held out his hands indicating the conversation was over. "I'm not telling you gentlemen anything yet. But I will." Ogie nodded to us and finished with, "I promise."

A light breeze brushed the leaves as we stalked through the woods like African hunters. Statues five times our age watched our movements through ivy-covered eyes. In the blackness of the November night, the figures seemed to be welcoming me to their home, long since vacant of visitors. We pushed through the pine limbs to the open space next to the road and crossed the bridge covering the fog filled stream that fed into the swamp. A deer bounced across the road and then two smaller deer followed. The bridge was dedicated to a woman and her baby who, in the 1950s, had driven off the bridge and drowned. The bridge was said to be haunted and, even though I heard nothing, a chill ran up my spine like the stealthy tap of death as I crossed the bridge and read the iron plaque.

We piled into Ogie's car and left the solitude of the swamped gardens. No one spoke on the drive back to town. Even in the quiet of the moment, I knew I would never be alone again. No words were needed to tell me that I had taken the final step to true friendship, the type of friendship that eludes some and that others only know in part. The only love we'd ever known had been from family and that came with baggage. We had yet to know the true love of a woman. This was the first love of our lives that came with no rules, no baggage and no expectations.

Chapter 2

The next morning, I woke up in the house I had lived in since birth. My parents were young and poor when they learned of the pregnancy and bought the house cheap in a rush to provide a place for a family, but they got what they paid for with a house that had holes in the ceiling, missing windows, and no working electricity. They had come from poverty so extreme it was almost unknown in America by my high school years. It was definitely unknown to me. Growing up penniless had taught them how to make something out of nothing and with their own hands they returned the house to its former glory one room at a time. My earliest memories include sitting on a mattress in the living room close to the fireplace for warmth, because my father had not yet installed heating. Other memories include the thrill of moving furniture into new rooms one room at a time after each had been restored and made livable again. The smell of paint and sawdust still brings a smile to my face.

I stepped out of my bed and dressed. I looked in my dresser mirror and frowned. Clothes didn't look good on my tall, thin and disproportional body. I had been almost six feet tall since seventh grade and never more than 130 pounds. I hated being referred to as the "skinny kid" as much as overweight kids hate being called fat, but people were less reluctant to comment on thinness. My brown hair curled to one side, making it impossible to style in any way but in a leaning wave that resembled a rolling hill of dead wheat. My blue eyes might have been an asset if it weren't for allergies that caused my eyes to turn red at the first hint of an allergen, and Georgians joked that 99 out of the 100 top allergen-producing plants and trees in the world were in Georgia, so my eyes were usually bloodshot giving me a perpetually stoned appearance.

I entered the kitchen and made myself a bowl of cereal. I guess there should be a nice description here about my mother cooking me french toast or scrambled eggs, but I can't include that because she was gone most of the time during my late teenage years.

My father couldn't replace her at the stove either as he was with her. Where were they? Maybe Charleston, maybe Nashville, maybe Miami, sometimes Chicago or New York. My parents and my little brother were gone most of the time—gone to places I'd never seen. The reason for their absence was my little brother Dante, a classical guitarist who was what many call a prodigy. And me, well, I was average.

Dante is four years younger than me and had been far from average for most of his life. Not long after turning one, he knew the alphabet and could count to twenty. Before he was three, he could read and perform simple math. His brain was developed far beyond that of even the brightest adults. While I struggled to draw my letters in the correct direction, he was performing feats of genius. Our parents took him to Emory University in Atlanta for special testing when he was two to see if he was truly gifted, and if so, how his gifts could be developed. That's when it was suggested by a team of Ph.D.s that he be introduced to music. It didn't take long for him to play beyond the talents of the local piano teacher, so he started taking guitar lessons from Stonewall Devine, a former rock star with a band who had two hit songs. Stonewall saw that Dante was a prodigy, something the piano teacher didn't, and introduced him to some music people in Nashville who set him up touring the country playing classical guitar.

And that's how it started. At first, Dante only played on weekends and in the summer at outdoor festivals, but as his talent developed, he started opening for classical bands, jazz bands, and even a few symphonies. By the time he was twelve, he was playing forty weeks of the year and making enough money for our parents to quit working and tour with him, while still saving enough for his future. My future was still undetermined, so no funds found their way to a trust for me, although I did get an allowance that was just enough to keep me from having to work after school. I was driving by the time Dante started touring and was almost as old as my parents were when they got married, so I was left all but on my own at sixteen. Almost alone anyway as there was always someone watching me within in the city limits. Everyone knew everyone in our small town and every mistake I made found its way back to my parents. This is why I learned to keep my activities stealthy and to abandon the city for the country roads around River Falls. As much as I would have liked to have had parties at my house, it wasn't to be. There was freedom to be found if one looked, but it took ingenuity, ingenuity that was natural to a teenager, but lost on adults.

I was proud of my brother's achievements, but also envious. Sometimes I was lonely, usually late at night, and I was often angry. Angry that my parents had left to travel the world with my little brother while leaving me to navigate my late teenage years alone. I still don't know why it took both of my parents to watch over my brother when one was enough. I guess the excitement of the road and the music business was too much for them to resist. They believed I could take care of myself, and I guess I did, but I really wanted them with me so I would have someone to talk to when I needed it. Even if the talks were the infrequent type common in teenage parent relationships.

After breakfast, I picked up the green Army pack I used to carry my books and pulled the straps over one shoulder. Wearing the pack correctly on both shoulders might be more ergonomically correct, but deducted cool points with every step, so I chose the less comfortable, back-destroying method.

The air was crisp and dry as I left my house on College Street and headed for school. I had walked this street a thousand times since boyhood, but I was still impressed with the perfection of the road. The homes had been built between 1880 and 1910, with

Victorian touches. Hundred year old oaks stood guard over the street and offered shade to the yards like big brothers protecting their kin. The homes were modest in size for the 1980s, but at the time they were built were owned by bankers, merchants, and other successful citizens of River Falls. Every house had a front porch, large windows and brick sidewalks. Some even had picket fences. Norman Rockwell couldn't have painted a more quintessential American street. My home was comfortable. A large porch with a two-person swing hung from the blue ceiling. Inside, large windows let light into twelve-foot high rooms. Every room had a fireplace, even though all but the one in the living room had been bricked over by my parents during restoration, but the mantels remained, adding history and art to every room but the kitchen and bathroom.

I walked by the court square and down to the corner. Here sat the Gem Movie Theater, a relic from the days of glorious movie houses. I remembered arriving late with my father to see Star Wars and walking into the theatre to view my first dogfight in space. I have no other stronger memory of a movie than the battle and explosions that took place on the Gem's giant screen. The theatre was the highlight of the town when it was built in the late 1920s, and it was the place to be on Friday night for years until a modern theatre opened in the early 1980s, forcing the outdated Gem Theater to close. The modern theatre didn't last either and closed during my freshman year in high school after it became a hangout for teenagers that never bought tickets.

I looked through the dusty windows of the Gem at the checkered floor and wished I could see a movie there again. When I was ten, my father explained to me that the balcony in the back of the theatre was for blacks. It seemed odd to me to separate people, but I had no opinion either way on the ethics of segregation, something that had ended only a few years before my birth. But the sixties was not my time and even though they shaped the world I lived in, they felt like a century before.

At the other end of the block, I passed Belton's Hardware Store, another place I visited with my father most often on Saturdays. With religious dedication, I always went to the stairwell leading to the basement to view a fish tank the size of a bathtub that contained an ugly gray fish the size of a football. I thought his name was Oscar, but now know that he was an Oscar type of fish. Maybe his name was Oscar too, I can't remember. While my father shopped for nails, I would stare at the fish and him back at me. With his thick, gray lips, he blew kisses and begged me with his eyes to take him home. He looked lonely, but this was his own fault because he ate everything that entered his lair.

The owner had reminded me to keep my fingers out of the water. "That fish'll bite your fingers off, son. You best keep 'em away from the tank." And I did.

Beyond the hardware store, I crossed the old iron bridge with flakes of red paint the size of plates that pulled back to reveal brown rust. Below the bridge was a twenty-foot deep canyon that hugged the railroad track that curved through town. Even the weight of my body caused the metal and wood to moan and pop like it was going to splinter at any moment. My mother feared the bridge so much that she refused to cross it in our car and would drive to the other end of town to avoid it. Many others felt the same way, as the only cars passing me on the bridge that morning were full of fearless teenagers racing to River Falls High School. I didn't usually walk, but my car, a 1966 Ford Mustang, was in the shop having the transmission replaced. I blew it out changing gears too fast trying to make the tires spin. A momentary, and very expensive, thrill.

In the distance, I heard a train approach, as it did every morning at the same time. I loved the sound of trains and their reliability. Just like the dull sound of the courthouse bell, the vibrations from trains and their horns comforted me. No matter how old I became, the trains and the bells remained the same – and I could count on them unlike most other things in my life. At night, the locomotives moved through the darkness like phantoms waking me only to a half-sleep so that I could hear their rumble and horns in the distance reminding me that I was warm in bed while others toiled.

Between the iron bridge and River Falls High, there were a few dozen of the most elegant antebellum style homes in Georgia, most with white columns the height of both floors. English Ivy spilled over dull granite and concrete walls that separated the sidewalk from the oak tree and magnolia-lined yards of the majestic mansions. In the spring, azaleas would fill the yards with white, pink and red blossoms boasting the fireworks of nature. I had walked and driven down this street so many times I could see in my mind the occupants of every house. I didn't know all their names, but had a memory of each one. You can't stay in the same place your entire life and not encounter almost everyone at least once. I remembered who had smiled as well as those who had motioned with their eyes for me to keep walking. The eye is a powerful tool used by aristocratic women of the South that can say more than a book full of words. Aristocratic women remained composed in public and would never be caught yelling at children in their yards like their more common Southern counterparts, but their silent threats were just as powerful.

Darwin was waiting for me as I approached the high school. Wearing his trademark black trench coat and Confederate kepi, he stood out among the students stuck in their starched oxfords and khaki pants or rock band t-shirts and stonewashed blue jeans. He could risk standing out without repercussion as his Dad was Sheriff Mayflower and highly respected in the community. He'd gotten me out of a bind or two over the years just as he had Ogie and Cassady.

"So, how does it feel?" Darwin asked as we crossed the green fescue lawn.

"What do you mean, how does it feel?" I asked.

"To be one of us? To be in the S.S.D.?" Darwin asked as he looked up at the windows in the second floor of the red brick building.

"It feels great, I guess. I never really knew if it even existed. 'Course, I already considered myself one of you, but thanks for reminding that I was the last one."

Darwin shrugged his shoulders and dismissed my concern.

We walked toward the front doors and I said, "Hey man, I'm sorry I laughed about that thing with Miescha…but you have to admit it's funny."

"Don't worry about it. It is sorta funny. I never really loved her anyway. I don't even believe in love. There's no such thing you know." Darwin stopped walking and looked toward the school. "There's only lust. That's it. Love isn't real. There's only lust."

Part of me believed he was saying this out of anger and humiliation, but I also thought that he might believe it, so I pushed him to learn more. "Really?" I said. "What about your parents? They seem really happy together."

"That's a different kind of love. Not much different from what you and I have—an admiration for each other, a deep friendship. It's comfortable and reliable. It's necessary, but it ain't love. Like I said, it's a lot like what we have, just more developed."

"Maybe, but we don't have sex."

"Neither do my parents," Darwin said, and looked at me with what was supposed to be a sexy come on face and whispered. "Not yet."

I laughed and then said, "Yeah, screw you man."

"Okay. If you want, but that'll just prove my point that there's no such thing as love, only lust."

I shook my head knowing he was using my words against me for his argument, even though it was in jest. "Well, if we have sex it won't be out of lust either. It will be something closer to what happens in prison."

"So you'd have sex with me if we were in prison together?" Darwin asked, and then put his hands on his waist akimbo and tapped his foot like he was impatiently waiting for an answer.

"Now that I think about it, I don't think prison would be enough."

"What if we were the last two people on earth?"

"Okay, maybe then, but only out of a responsibility to repopulate the earth."

"Hey you two. Come over here and see me," Elena yelled to us from the wall of the school building. I hadn't seen her during our conversation. "What are you two talking about it? It looks serious."

"We're talking about the world population crisis," I said as we approached her. Darwin laughed and Elena looked confused as she held her books with both hands in front of her while leaning on one shoulder against the brick wall.

"Okay, boys. And they say girls are hard to understand."

Elena Luna was from a family of Argentinian immigrants. Her family moved to our small town a dozen years before and opened a restaurant. Argentinian cuisine failed, so they opened a Mexican restaurant, The La Siesta. The double use of "the" was no mistake. They thought it was funny, but few locals seemed to catch the joke except for the high school Spanish teacher who wasted no less than ten hours per semester protesting to her students about the grammar error and the damage the restaurant's name was doing to the Latino culture.

The Lunas hired a staff of Mexican immigrant cooks and a few Hispanics for the wait staff to give the restaurant ambiance and to make it believable as a Mexican restaurant.

They hit gold when they added an arcade and started playing music popular with the kids in high school. Of course they still threw in a Mariachi band occasionally, but that only added to the allure.

Elena looked at me and I felt my chest tighten. Elena's dark eyes pierced the heart of every boy in school. Her long dark hair held playful curls from a perm months before; her body was strong, clean, and pure as a mountain spring. She was the girl you took home to meet your parents, if you could ever get up the courage to ask her out in the first place.

"Hey boys. Whatcha up to?"

"About 5'11"," I responded and then thought to myself, did I really just tell that stupid joke to the prettiest girl in school?

"About, the uh, ah, about the same here." Darwin tripped over his words as he stumbled in her beauty.

"You two are so silly," she said, then giggled. "Hey Darwin. My mother asked about you. She wants you to come by the restaurant. She's got something for your mother."

"Ok, yeah, I'll come by after school today. Are you going to be there?" Darwin tried to look into her eyes when he spoke, but his nerves won and his gaze shifted to the wall behind her.

Elena curled her hair around her finger. "I'll be there."

The first bell rang and Elena went inside the building while Darwin and I continued around the side of the building to avoid the hall crowds.

"You like her don't you?" I asked.

He stopped, breathed in through his mouth then curled his bottom lip as the air exhaled through his nose. "How can I not?

She's hotter than hell—the best looking girl in school as far as I'm concerned. But man, there's no way she'd go for me."

"I don't know why you say that. You're a cool guy. You stand out as much as she does."

"Is that a compliment?" He asked.

I laughed and then responded, "Yeah, it is a compliment. You should ask her out."

"I can't stand another rejection right now. What if she just really likes me as a friend? What if my asking her out makes things awkward and causes her to act weird around me? What if my asking her out screws up everything? What if I freak her out?"

"So what? If that's it, then you two will just become better friends. She won't freak out. I promise."

Darwin took his Confederate kepi off and said, "I don't know. Maybe. Probably not."

"Just think of it this way: if you two are the last two people on earth, she'll be a lot more fun to repopulate with than me."

Our first class was theatre. When we arrived, Yonah was sitting on the stage next to Ogie. Yonah had been my off and on girlfriend since kindergarten and always my personal friend. When I say 'girlfriend,' I really mean close friend whom I sometimes kissed and often held hands with, but it was little more than one of those deep admirations Darwin talked about. Girls were an enigma to me and I usually followed their lead. If the girl wanted to make out, I made out; if they wanted to break up, we broke up. I had no idea how the game of love, or even lust, was supposed to be played. I played it like a rookie hobo trying to jump on a moving train while doing my best not to fall under the wheels. So far I'd fallen under the wheels every time.

When Darwin saw the others, he raised his hand in the air and made the popular heavy metal sign of the horns with his fingers. Or so I thought.

"Dude, you just said you love me in sign language," Ogie yelled across the room.

"Oh, well. You know I do. And uh, rock on!"

I sat next to Yonah, who immediately reached over and put her hand on mine. She smiled and looked at me but said nothing.

Her smile was forced and I knew why. Her mother, Dr. Cook, had been fighting Lou Gehrig's disease, also known as ALS, for several years and it was obvious that she was within the last months of her life. Dr. Cook was the first and only person I had ever known with Lou Gehrig's disease, but if anyone was going to get an exotic illness it was Yonah's mother who was never one to follow the rules: the rules of society, of life, or the rules the old South imposed on women. As a successful doctor, she waited until her mid-thirties to have a child and when she did it, it was without the help of a husband—not past the insemination part anyway. Yonah didn't know her father and her mother's independence led many to believe the father didn't know he had a daughter. This arrangement had worked well enough in Yonah's childhood, but now with her mother dying and no family Yonah would be alone.

"Hey guys. Make sure to clap loud after my skit," Darwin requested as he walked toward the stage. The teacher motioned for us to sit down, so we found seats.

Darwin walked behind the curtain at the edge of the stage, brought out a gray boom box, walked to the center of the stage, pressed play and raised the boom box above his head in a manner inspired by the movie Say Anything. His version wasn't a love song, but The Beatles "Revolution." The song blasted throughout the room as Darwin gazed like a soldier at the back of the room, not making eye contact with anyone. His face was solemn, his body tense. The song played through and, at the end, he walked the boom box back to the curtain and returned to his seat with us.

No one clapped. We were beyond clapping as we had just witnessed a happening.

"Thanks a lot, assholes," Darwin said as he returned to his seat.

"For what?" Ogie asked.

"For sitting there like frogs on a log. Why didn't you clap like I asked?"

Yonah leaned over me to Darwin, put her hand on his cheek and whispered just loud enough for us all to hear. "Because we just witnessed something special and unique." Then she kissed him for several seconds. She was holding my hand and kissing my best friend. I really didn't understand women.

I was seven when I first met Yonah. She moved into a house on a street parallel to mine. A trail ran through the woods between the streets with occasional arteries that connected the trail to the backyards where child explorers lived. Sometimes teenagers used the woods between the houses to smoke pot and make out, but mostly it was a place of adventure for those not yet old enough to drive or that cared to get stoned. Yonah and her mother were walking the trail when I saw them through the trees.

"Hello, what are you doing in my woods?" I questioned them like a police officer who had just stumbled upon a robbery in progress.

"Oh, are we in your woods?" Dr. Cook asked holding up her hands in surrender.

"Yes, those are my woods. If I don't know you, you can't walk in them."

"Well then, we must meet," Dr. Cook responded while walking from the main trail toward my yard. "This is my daughter, Yonah. We just moved into a house through the woods. My name is Dr. Cook." She held out her hand and I cautiously accepted her shake.

"Nice to meet you," I said.

"Would you mind if Yonah came over to play sometimes?" Dr. Cook asked.

"Nope."

"Right to the point. I like a man that doesn't beat around the bush."

"Yep, and you can use my woods all you like, now that I know you and all."

"Well, thank you." Dr. Cook smiled. "And what is your name young man?"

"My name is Augustus Longfellow Ambrose. That's a lot to say so everyone just calls me Gus."

"Okay then, Gus. We'll see you around." And with that, my friendship with Yonah Cook began.

I had never had a true friend before she wandered into my yard and I appreciated every moment I spent with her. While most boys my age were playing backyard football or baseball, I was sitting under a tree drawing or playing in the dirt with toy soldiers.

I hated sports and would rather sit alone in my yard than throw a football back and forth like a dog chasing a stick. Yonah was a girl and I soon learned the value of a playmate with little enthusiasm for helmets and baseball gloves.

With Yonah, I learned to notice and appreciate the little things that made up the world and made the world beautiful. She would find splendor in a beetle as easily as a butterfly. She enjoyed the hottest of days and the coldest with equal zeal. While our parents were complaining of the stifling humidity of August or the icy winds of February, she was noticing the changing colors and shapes of the sky. Yonah laughed at my jokes, even when they were not funny. Not out of sympathy, but because she found the humor in even the most subtle gestures. She was my first real friend when the biggest differences between boys and girls was limited to clothing and bathrooms.

On some Saturdays I would enjoy tea with Yonah and Dr. Cook. The doctor told me that one should always make time for tea in the afternoon because the act showed your problems that they were not so important they couldn't wait. Dr. Cook practiced general medicine in an old house just outside of town. She rarely had to deal with emergencies and this gave her the luxury of shutting down her office every afternoon for tea with her staff when they would retreat to an old brick patio beneath a giant hundred-year-old oak with rolling roots the size of Amazon pythons that caused the bricks to rise and fall in red waves. The iron tables and chairs were too heavy to blow away in storms and so durable they had probably been there as long as the house.

Yonah and I tried to be in the same classes at school and she'd invite me to church, where we'd sit together and she would kick my feet and sometimes tickle me, hoping I'd laugh during prayer.

"She has a crush on you," my father told me once after she gave me a handmade Valentine's Day card.

I disagreed. We were best friends and I couldn't imagine ever going with a best friend. The concepts of friendship and love mixed as well as oil and water in my mind.

It was late August in 1982 when she kissed me for the first time. We were hiding in an igloo of vines when she grabbed my face with her dirty hands and kissed me on the mouth.

"What the…why did you do that?" I asked her. I wasn't sure if I was disgusted or happy.

"I did it cause I like you dummy."

"Oh."

"You're the first boy I ever kissed. Do you know that?"

I didn't; I wasn't sure I believed her. After taking a few seconds to digest what had just happened, I decided I liked it. "You're the first girl to ever kiss me. Did you know that?" I flirted for the first time in my life and felt a tingle in my hair.

"That can't be right. You must of kissed lots of girls."

Was she joking, I wondered?

"No, no you're the first," I whispered to her as I worked the flirtation.

"I think we should do that again sometime," she said.

"How about now?" I asked while looking at her with my head cocked to the side.

"No, I think that's enough for now. We'll kiss again later."

She had my heart after that, but I was too shy to ever tell her, so I left her a white rose on her bicycle the first Valentine's Day after our kiss. I left other white roses for her to find on her birthdays and when good things happened to her, like winning the sixth grade spelling bee. I never told her it was me, but she knew because she would always talk about her secret admirer and tell me how happy the flowers made her.

Yonah always saw the art in everything. Even things that weren't supposed to be art, like her mother dying. Yeah, that's right. The pretty girl with blond hair and blue eyes I'd been friends with since I was a kid was now a ward of River Falls because her mother had lost all ability to move her legs, lost some movement in her arms and was starting to lose the ability to breathe on her own. Her mother had been diagnosed with the disease when we were in junior high school and now the disease was taking final control. Somehow, Yonah found the positive in this.

A few months before, she had told me, "At least I know my mother's dying. I get to tell her all the things people don't get to say when someone dies suddenly. My mother knows what she means to me and I know what I mean to her. It's beautiful to have a disease that gives you a chance to set things right."

The judge that ran the probate allowed Yonah to live with her mother. Old Judge Rush had been the probate judge in Caswell County, the county of River Falls, for over forty years. His job consisted of verifying election results, handing out birth certificates, dealing with estates after deaths and occasionally appointing lawyers to oversee children who had lost parents or whose parents had abandoned them. Most people in River Falls believed Old Judge Rush was suffering from senility, but since only Republican candidates won elections and he only had to sign off on birth certificates, few saw a real reason to replace him, so Rush continued to hold his elected position despite doing odd things like wearing two different colors of shoes and rarely zipping his pants fly.

The judge's mental infirmity might have been laughable if not for a serious mistake when he placed a despicable lawyer in charge of overseeing Yonah, her mother and Dr. Cook's financial estate. The Judge had fallen under the spell of a lawyer who had graduated from Lucifer Law College and climbed out of the pits of Hell to practice law in the small Southern town of River Falls. In truth, the lawyer, Taft E. Gregory, had graduated from a respectable New England university, but I dare not tarnish the name of the school by mentioning it in the same paragraph as T.E. Gregory. I've been told there is good in everyone, and this must be true because some people in town liked him, but I would never see or know of this good.

Gregory was only thirty and in the first years of his practice when Old Judge Rush appointed him. Gregory started working in real estate law, but changed direction when he found that he preferred those being prosecuted more than families buying houses, and became a defense attorney. He knew the local D.A. and knew they were too overworked to properly prosecute everyone, so he found ways to get the slimiest pedophiles, suspected murderers and others with sociopathic tendencies off. Later Gregory jumped on the opportunity to manage personal estates as a guardian when he realized it was easy money. Most wards could be placed in a nursing home while Gregory took a percentage of every dime spent for their care. The more he spent, the more he made. It was a simple and workable formula for a quick and easy fortune, not to mention any funds that could be siphoned off through other means that were legal but highly unethical. It was the job of the probate judge to protect wards from unscrupulous lawyers, but the judge was too inept to do much more than process birth certificates.

Yonah suspected Gregory was stealing from her mother on top of the high fees he was already taking, but she had no way to prove it. She tried to hire an accountant to audit her mother's financial accounts, but Gregory blocked funds for her to hire the accountant and claimed the audit was "baseless and unnecessary." He told the judge that any audits would only deplete the funds that were needed to take care of Dr. Cook. Yonah set up meetings with the judge and the lawyer but Gregory never showed up to any of the meetings and the judge was too far under the spell of the sycophant and too invested in Gregory to argue with him about missing meetings. Any anger he might have had for Taft would diminish when he picked the judge up for their weekly lunch at the old barbeque restaurant just outside of town. Judge Rush also happened to be an old golfing buddy with Taft's father, which established an immediate relationship between the two. A relationship Taft E. Gregory exploited like a grandson working a grandparent for inheritance.

Yonah's mother was dying, dying of a disease that was taking her slowly and painfully. The same judge that had signed Yonah's birth certificate had placed an evil soul to oversee her and her mother. Her life was as difficult as any I knew, yet she was always smiling. I thought nothing could ever break her.

Chapter 3

"You going to tell us about your imaginary girlfriend Ogie, or are we gonna have to follow you around till we catch you with her?" Cassady asked as we drove toward Gethsemane.

"Yeah, come on. It's time you spilled the beans on your secret babe," I said, hoping Ogie would finally tell us about his lover.

For months Ogie had been seeing a girl, but we didn't know who. When I say we didn't know who she was, I mean we really didn't know anything about her. His parents didn't know and I'm sure the girl's parents didn't know either. Why would anyone keep a girl secret? We didn't care what she looked like. At least that's what we told him.

"Look man, if she's ugly that's ok too. In fact, it's in your best interest if she is ugly. At least then you don't have to worry about Darwin stealing her from you," I said, hoping for a laugh.

"She's not ugly. She's beautiful." Ogie gazed out the foggy window as a light rain started to trickle down the glass. "Darwin says there's no such thing as love. Maybe he's right, but this is something. I think about her day and night."

"Then why not introduce us?" Darwin asked. "She's fat isn't she? She's like 600 pounds. Did you find her on Oprah? You did, didn't you? We'll still love her, you know. We love fat girls. Isn't that right Cassady?"

"Shut up Darwin," Cassady yelled.

"No, I didn't find her on TV, and she's not fat. I haven't told y'all because I didn't think y'all would understand."

"What's to understand? She's a girl…right?" I asked. "Oh shit. You're gay. You're gay, aren't you? Your dad's gonna kill you."

Ogie forced a laugh. "Yeah man, she's a girl. I'm not gay," Ogie said and then mumbled, "She's black. She's a black girl."

Time froze as we held our breath, not knowing how to respond. As progressive as we considered ourselves, we knew few who had gone outside their race to date and none to marry. I can't tell you why it was odd for us, as we were Americans and already a mix of various nationalities and blood lines, except maybe for Ogie who was pure English to his bones. We no longer lived in the Old South of our grandparents, but we didn't live in New York City either. It wasn't just taboo in our mutt white world, but in the black world as well. Our parents taught us that segregation was wrong, to never use the infamous "N" word and to be as friendly to black folks as we were to anyone else, but there was also an unspoken law against getting too close to "black folks" and them to us. Separate but equal felt like a workable idea from our perspective and we saw no fault in the concept; we knew not of the pain it caused, but now the world was beyond separate but equal as we were the first generation integrated our entire lives in school. The only physical reminders of a separate world survived in the second floor of the Gem Movie Theatre which was once the only place blacks were allowed and on separate plaques on the memorial at the courthouse for Whites and 'Colored' who had served in the Great War. There were also stories from our parents about segregation, something that felt as far in the past as the Civil War. All was equal on the surface, but there was an invisible line that wasn't crossed. Now our best friend had broken the law. He had crossed the invisible line.

When people found out, Ogie was going to get attention. I thought about how he was used to attention, but for different reasons. Everywhere Ogie went, he stood out among crowds— sometimes because of his social status and always for his physical presence. Several inches taller than most high school kids, he demanded respect. I was six feet tall and my eyes were level with his chin. His shoulders were so large they pushed his head slightly forward. His face was part aristocrat and part savage—a combination of good breeding and generations of hard men had created a Southern man with an edge. His hair was thick and curly and, if uncut for more than a few weeks, would grow out in all directions, giving him the appearance of a child raised by wolves, so he usually kept it cropped close in an almost military style.

Ogie favored khaki pants that were too large and sagged so low his boxers were often visible. He could wear an oxford better than anyone, but preferred worn out t-shirts that were soft and comfortable but better suited for washing cars than wearing.

Genetics and the pressure to succeed had created a boy who was smarter than most men. He didn't have the experience and wisdom to back up his brains, but no one could beat him in a debate, or should I say verbal fight as he excelled in all manners of combat both physical and mental. He once made a teacher cry because he wouldn't back down from his argument that koala bears were carnivorous. I looked it up after class and found that he was wrong, but I didn't see the point in arguing the fact with him because I knew he'd win even if I showed him the encyclopedia. He would convince me that the encyclopedia, researched and written by a team of Ph.D.s was incorrect, thus leaving me with questions about the validity of a U.S. written document about an Australian miniature bear.

My desire to avoid verbal fights with Ogie was probably another foundation of our friendship and I think he returned the favor by not mocking me when I made obvious errors in grammar or redneckish comments.

When I met Ogie, he was the ultimate rebel. We were ten and I was attending one of my regular Cub Scout meetings.

"Where are that guy's parents," I thought as a kid with wild hair low crawled under the front row of seated Cub Scouts. I tried to ignore the wild child, but this became impossible when he untied my shoelace and started tying it to the foot of my chair.

"Stop it," I whispered.

He looked up at me and laughed, but made no attempt to muffle his laughter.

"Get off the floor. Get back in your seat. The scout master is going to get mad," I said, again whispering.

His eyes grew wide and I was sure I had convinced him to return to his seat, but a shadow behind alerted me to the presence of an adult. The boy stood up, almost knocking me out of my seat, and then ran between the chairs and out the back door. All the scouts turned around to see the wild haired boy running out the back door with the shadow in pursuit (his mother, I realized). The lady apologized to everyone as she walked quickly toward the door. An explosion of glass from the hallway, followed by screams from the boy, ended the meeting. Most parents in attendance remained in their seats, but the scout master and every Cub Scout launched toward the hallway to inspect the damage and see for himself what had occurred.

"You're done with Scouts young man. You're never leaving your house again," the boy's mother scolded.

"But I didn't do anything," the wild child responded and then kicked a piece of glass away from his feet.

"What? What are you talk...talking about...you...you just busted a glass case wide open. A church display case no less. Ge...get...get in the car. Go now... get in the car now." The mother's face was red and her eyes as wild as the boy's hair. The mother turned to the scout master who was looking at the broken glass. "I'm sorry. Conrad doesn't usually act like this. I think he drank some red Kool-Aid. He gets wild when he consumes red dye number six. We'll pay for the damages."

"What?" Conrad asked as his brow tightened.

"What...what do you mean Conrad? Shut your mouth."

"I'm sorry mother, I cannot. We will not pay for the damages. This case was clearly in my way and if anyone needs to pay for damages, it's the church. I'm a child and this is an unsafe environment," Conrad Oglethorpe said before his mother grabbed him by the arm and pulled him out the door to the parking lot.

The wild child was dragged to his car and was about to climb into the back seat when I ran out and met him. "My name is Gus. I guess your name is Conrad," I said.

"Yeah, but I don't like Conrad. You can call me Ogie. I made that name up myself and I think it's great."

"Can you make up your own nickname?" I asked before seeing the boy's mother slam her head against the steering wheel.

"Yeah you can," he responded not seeming to notice his mother's breakdown.

"How do you know?" I asked. "I've never heard of anyone making up their nickname. I don't think you're supposed to."

"I know you can do it because I just did. I made up my own nickname so that means it can be done."

He had a point, and that's how I met Ogie and also when I learned that an argument with him couldn't be won. I had never seen anyone my age defy adults and authority with such style before and I was captivated. The next day, I found the only Conrad in the Scout directory and called his house.

"Ogie, this is Gus from Cub Scouts. Whatcha doin' this weekend? My mother said I could have company over."

"I would like to come over, but my mother won't let me leave the house. I'm grounded." There was a pause. "I have an idea. I'll invite you over for the night and when you show up with your parents, my mother will be too embarrassed to send you home. Bring your camping gear and fishing pole and we'll camp by the Majestic Lakes in the woods behind my house."

Ogie was right. His mother didn't send me away. With customary Southern charm, she welcomed my parents into their large antebellum home. I knew the white-columned mansion well. My father enjoyed long country drives on the weekends and we often drove by the River Falls landmark that sat a quarter mile from Cotton Field Rd. The driveway was lined with magnolia trees that sprung from thick azalea bushes that bloomed pink and white every spring. The old plantation home sat at the edge of woods that were lined with dogwood trees that opened their white flowers before the magnolias and contrasted with the yellow daffodils that filled the rolling fields around the mansion. The field in front of the house was once a cotton field, as were the fields across the street from the mansion that were now horse stables and riding pastures. Next to the house was a rolling cow pasture that was once part of the plantation as well, but had been owned by a cattle rancher since the Oglethorpe family sold off their land decades before after not using it for years.

"Please come in. Can I get you something to drink?" Mrs. Oglethorpe asked my parents.

Before we arrived, my parents had told me they were in a hurry, but it would be rude to refuse a drink, so they accepted. "Sure, we'll have whatever you have ready," my father said.

"Excellent. I'll get you something now. I'm sorry the help isn't here today. We try to give them the weekends off."

"Of course," my mother responded like we had a maid and understood the kindness in letting the help off on weekends. "Gus, why don't you go outside and get your camping and fishing gear."

"Fishing and camping?" Mrs. Oglethorpe dealt with the surprise of my visit, but hadn't anticipated her son taking to the woods for the night. But to admit she didn't know of Ogie's plans would be admitting to defeat, so she turned her shocked face into a happy one. Ogie knew of her desire to always maintain composure and played it to his advantage.

"Yes, mother. I told you we were going to camp by the lakes."

"Yes, yes, of course you did." And with that Ogie and I were free.

"I'll pick you up tomorrow afternoon," I heard my father say as I ran into the woods with Ogie.

The price to be paid by the lead person clearing the spider webs from the trees is that you get hit with every limb as the leader pushes through. Ogie was a natural in the woods and, even though there was a gravel road and a trail from his house to the Majestic Lakes, he chose the shortest path—straight through the woods. In Georgia, the woods are thick. They are thick with briars, poison ivy, small trees, medium-sized trees and large trees. In between the trees and bushes are spider webs hoping to catch some of the millions of mosquitoes and biting flies that zoom looking for blood from Cub Scouts.

"Hurry up, Gus. I want to get our tent set up so we can start fishing. There's a giant catfish in the big lake named Moby. I hope to catch him. If I don't, I might drain the lake and just pick him up off the bottom."

"How do you drain a lake?" I asked.

"You blow up the dam," he responded without hesitation.

When we reached the twin lakes I was impressed. "I can't believe no one lives next to these lakes." The matching lakes were separated by dirt just wide enough for a car to drive between them, or a wagon as was probably first intended. There was one visible road that lead back to Ogie's house, but it was covered in grass and a large tree had fallen making it impossible to reach by vehicle, but still accessible on foot. I hoped we would return via the road in the morning.

"The lakes were man-made back around the turn of the century, but no one has used the area for fun stuff since the fifties, except for occasional fishermen like us," Ogie said as he swiped at a mosquito flying around his forehead. "There's a bunch of rusty signs and the frames from a few of the old buildings. It's like a ghost town. The last time I camped out here, my dad scared the shit outta me by hiding in one of the old cabins and running out with a cranked chainsaw. I nearly fainted." Ogie turned and smiled at me while mimicking a chainsaw with his fishing rod.

"I hope he doesn't do that tonight," I said with fear that he actually might.

"I don't think he will. He's going hunting tomorrow morning, so he'll be up early."

"Does he hunt around here?" I asked.

"Sometimes. He probably won't since he knows we're camping out here."

"That's good. I don't want to get shot."

"That probably won't happen. Don't be a sissy."

"Okay. I just don't want to get shot," I mumbled to myself.

We set up our A-frame tent between a collapsed cabin and the lake nearest the earthen dam. Dark brown wood skeletons of several structures remained and an old gas station sign was leaning against one framed building laid on a rock foundation. Our campsite was clear of trees and offered a large area of soft grass with a rock fire pit. Two stumps sat next to the fire pit.

"Are you staying in Cub Scouts?" I asked.

"What do you think?" Ogie said and spit into the fire pit.

"I don't think they'll let you back in, but maybe another pack will."

"It doesn't matter. My mother was madder than a rattlesnake. My dad was an Eagle Scout and they want me to become one too. I like being outside, but I don't see much need in going Eagle."

"I like Scouts," I said.

"I like this lake," Ogie said. "Let's catch some fish."

That night we ate catfish fried in butter and wild onion. The taste of an animal you catch, clean, and cook can't be compared to anything else. Maybe it's the instinct to hunt and kill that makes prey taste so good. Maybe it's just the freshness. In the South, we believe that anything that tastes good tastes better fried and our meal that night was a feast for royalty.

Ogie raised his metal Army canteen and said, "I want to make a toast, a toast to the Majestic Lakes."

I raised my Cub Scout canteen and then drank before making my own toast.

"I want to make a toast too. I want to toast this tasty fish that is now swimming in my belly."

We laughed.

"Want to go to the old mine and catch bats?" Ogie asked.

"Old mine? You have an old mine?"

"Yeah, it's on my family's land. Well, land that used to be my family's. The mines haven't been used for years. My grandfather sold the land to a mining company, but they didn't find anything and abandoned them a few years later. I'm not supposed to go into them, but I do sometimes."

"Okay, let's do it, but how do we catch bats?" I asked.

"We'll have to sneak back to my house and get a jar."

We doused the campfire with water from the lake and then walked the old dirt road back to Ogie's house. Lights from the mansion were visible hundreds of yards away, even through the thick trees. Ogie's parents added a pool to the antebellum home's backyard and a large patio for entertaining. Bright lights lit the patio and pool even though it was almost midnight. I knew they were rich because my dad would never have allowed unused lights to remain on during the night. The back door to the kitchen was unlocked. We took our muddy shoes off, left them at the door and walked into a pantry the size of my bedroom.

"Boys, what are you doing?"

I turned quickly to see Mr. Oglethorpe. He was wearing a maroon colored robe, had a book under his arm and an unlit pipe in his mouth. "Aren't you boys supposed to be camping? Raiding the pantry at midnight isn't exactly living off the land." He smiled at us.

"Yes sir. We are getting a jar to catch stuff in the woods. We ate catfish for dinner."

"Are you really taking that jar, son? That's your mother's favorite jar, you know."

Ogie looked at the jar and held it up for his father to take. "Okay. We won't take it."

"I don't want it son. Just take care of it. Jars are very valuable around here. I don't know what your mother's fascination is with used jars, but if you lose it, I'll hear about it for months."

"Dad, can we take a couple of guns with us too?"

"Sure, that's fine."

"Yes sir."

We carried two shotguns from the columned mansion over our shoulders like Confederate soldiers leaving to protect the South from Northern aggression. I waited until the lights of the house were no longer visible and asked Ogie about his guns. "Your parents don't mind if you shoot without them around?"

"Nah, they don't mind. We've always had guns. It's a birthright my dad says. It's a Second Amendment right."

I nodded my head, but had no idea what the Second Amendment was. "My dad takes me shooting a lot, but he doesn't let me keep any guns in my room. He keeps them locked up," I said.

Ogie shrugged his shoulders and said, "My parents won't let me have a motorcycle, but they give me all the guns I want. I asked them for a motorcycle last Christmas and they told me I'd only kill myself. They got me this twelve-gauge instead."

The open mines were dark and I couldn't see the bottom of the first pit until I leaned over the edge and shined my flashlight into the hole. There was a rope tied to a nearby tree that was coiled like a sleeping rat snake. Ogie let out some of the rope and dropped the rest over the side. The hole was twenty feet deep and ten feet in diameter. I followed Ogie down the rope with some hesitation, but none I would show. We dropped to the bottom and landed on the wet leaves that felt like a water-logged mattress that had been left on the side of the road. At the bottom were two forty-five degree vertical tunnels that were three feet wide and only four feet high. Ogie gathered the rope and tossed it down one shaft.

"How far down does that go?" I asked.

"Not too far, maybe twenty feet. I think it used to go a lot deeper, but the shaft collapsed. My dad said it went a hundred feet when he was a boy. He said digging this tunnel was a futile attempt at getting rich quick."

"What does futile mean?" I asked Ogie.

"I think it means fucking stupid."

That sounded about right to me and I was glad to learn a new word. "Do you have the jar?" I asked.

Ogie laughed and then said, "Yes, but we must be careful 'cause it's my mother's favorite jar."

We didn't have to bend over far when we entered the tunnel because we were not much taller than the height of the cave. Water dripped from the ceiling, wetting our hair with its musty cologne. Leaves made the path slippery and we used the rope to keep from slipping down the hole like a water slide. When we neared the bottom, Ogie dropped to the tunnel floor and motioned for me to do the same. He took the jar from his backpack, handed me the lid and held the container above his head as he examined the ceiling like a mechanic looking for leaks. He smiled, and looked at me at the same time, he pointed to a dark blob attached to the dirt above us.

Ogie took the jar, placed it over the bat and then moved the jar to the side so that the mammal fell into the jar. I immediately put the lid over the mouth of the jar and screwed it on tightly. The bat fluttered and bounced off the glass in all directions, looking for an escape. It was likely this animal had never encountered humans before and her first encounter was met with tragedy.

"You want to take it home with you?" Ogie asked.

"Yeah, I'll have to hide it from my mother, but I know a good place."

"Okay, but don't tell her I gave it to you. You'll have to make something up if she asks."

"I'll tell her I got it at a bat store."

"That's right. Tell her that. And don't forget to bring my mother's jar back before she finds out it's missing."

I took the bat home and hid her in the laundry room in a mason jar from my house. I covered the mouth of the jar with a piece of an old t-shirt and secured it with a rubber band. I was sure that would hold the animal, but when I returned later to feed the bat, the rubber band had popped loose and the bat was free. I never found the bat and assumed it had found a way out of the laundry room.

A year later my mother found a bat skeleton behind the washing machine during her spring cleaning. When she asked me about it, I shrugged my shoulders.

We stayed up late into the night and awoke when the sun created a greenhouse effect, heating the tent to an uncomfortable level. A brown spider crawled over Ogie's sleeping bag and onto his shotgun. His eyes opened when I reached over him and killed the spider with my shoe. The impact jammed several legs between the wooden butt and the main body of the gun. Yellow guts oozed over the oiled metal.

Ogie looked at the bug guts and laughed. "That's so gross. Uuuugggghhh."

"I know. I didn't think he would bust up like that," I said.

"Hey, you want to shoot some snakes?" Ogie asked me.

"Snakes? Where will we find them? Do you have a snake pit too?"

"Sort of, yeah. The creeks behind the lakes are full of moccasins," Ogie said.

The cold water took my breath and tightened my stomach when I stepped from the bank into the creek. Clay made the sides slippery and the creek walls moved above us as we waded upstream through the slow moving, murky water. We followed the creek until it stopped at a beaver pond surrounded by a grassy bank. The water was now up to our waists, so we kept the shotguns against our shoulders with the barrels pointed skyward.

"Alright, Gus. This is where you gotta be careful. This pond is full of old and mean moccasins. My father told me to stay the hell away from here."

"Do you think he'll get mad if he catches us here?" I asked.

"How's he going to catch us? Look where we're at." Ogie stopped quickly in the water and held up his left hand behind him, making a fist. I stopped and looked down at the water to see a fat snake swimming through the water in front of Ogie. It was less than three feet long, but his diamond shaped head and dark gray body made him appear much larger and more sinister. Ogie lowered his shotgun and pointed it at the snake which was only a few feet in front of us. He cocked his weapon, stopped his breathing and slowly pulled back on the trigger. Fire and lead shot from his gun, hitting the water with an impact that sent droplets into our faces and eyes. The snake was propelled into the air with us scurrying to get out from under its landing zone. The snake hit the now rippling beaver pond with a slap. Ogie looked over at the snake like he was looking over a wall when the moccasin opened its mouth, showing us its fangs and white cotton-colored mouth.

"Oh shit!" I screamed, as I moved quickly backwards through the water.

Out of fear or aggression, the reptile pursued us through the water, but with much greater efficiency. We didn't know if it was chasing us or confused and trying to escape, but we did know it would be more than pleased to sink its venom filled teeth into our skin. The snake passed Ogie and swam for me. The moccasin opened its mouth and lifted to bite my back when Ogie grabbed the tail of my attacker, pulling it quickly from the water. Before it could right itself, Ogie threw the snake toward the shore, where it hit a tree and fell to the ground. I pointed my shotgun at the snake, put my finger on the trigger and squeezed off a shot that sent a dozen small lead pellets into the snake. The animal thrashed on the ground for several seconds and died.

"Man, did you see that?" I asked Ogie, turning around in the water to thank him. "Thanks for grabbing that sucker. He almost..." I stopped talking when I saw expanding red spots on Ogie's t-shirt.

Ogie's eyes started to roll back in his eye sockets when he fell towards me. I grabbed him and walked him out of the water and sat him next to a tree a few feet from the dead snake.

"Ogie, Ogie? Are you okay?" I asked, laying my shotgun on the ground. "You okay man?" I felt my eyes filling with tears.

"What...what are you...are you crying man?" Ogie asked while looking at me with the combined sarcasm of a ten-year-old boy and the pain of a wounded soldier. "I think the birdshot bounced off the water and hit me."

"Yeah, that's what happened I think."

"Is it bad? I'm afraid to look. Did I ruin my shirt? My mom's going to be so mad."

"Yeah man, your shirt is ruined. You have about ten pieces of shot in your chest. We don't have anything to wrap around you to stop the bleeding. We need to get you home," I said thinking that Ogie might die in the swamp, leaving me to find a way out and to return his dead body to his family.

Ogie pulled his shirt off, smearing blood across his cheeks and forehead. I took his shirt and wiped blood away from each gunshot wound. I was relieved when I saw that most of the lead pieces were visible just under his skin.

"It doesn't look too bad, but you're going to have to stay focused so you don't pass out. I learned in Cub Scouts what to do if you go into shock, so tell me if you do," I said making Ogie smile. I then realized what I had said. "Well, don't go into shock or pass out or anything. Just don't do it."

Mr. Oglethorpe was chopping wood in the yard when we walked from the trees. I had left the shotguns next to the beaver pond because I couldn't carry them and help Ogie at the same time. I quietly watched Mr. Oglethorpe's muscular arms vibrate when he hit the wood with his ax. Ogie and I approached him from behind. He didn't see us and continued to blast away at the wood. I couldn't make my mouth say the words, "your son has been shot," so I stood there hoping he would turn around, or that some sort of divine intervention would end the moment. Ogie ended it for me.

"Dad... Dad. I messed up."

Mr. Oglethorpe stopped cutting and turned to see his son covered in blood from face to waist. Seconds felt like minutes as he estimated the damage and processed what had happened. He looked at me for an answer, but my mouth wouldn't move so I looked to the ground embarrassed.

"Dad, I fired into the water and the shot ricocheted into my chest. I don't think it's as bad as it looks." Ogie tried to smile to show his father he was not as seriously injured as he appeared. "I guess we need to go to the doctor."

Mr. Oglethorpe carried Ogie into the house and brought him to his office. The last time the old wooden floors of the office had seen blood was when the room was used by surgeons in the Civil War to amputate arms and legs from both Confederate and Union soldiers. The surgeons selected the room because the window opened to the side of the house, where cut limbs could be tossed out and buried. He sat Ogie in a rocking chair passed down from his great grandmother. Ogie relaxed and his head fell against the chair.

"No son of mine is going to the doctor for doing something stupid," Mr. Oglethorpe said as he left the room. He returned a minute later with a stack of towels, a bottle of hydrogen peroxide, a bottle of acetaminophen, a sharp knife from the kitchen, and a pair of tweezers. "I can get the shot out, but you're going to have to be tough, son. Do you understand me?" he asked, looking into Ogie's frightened eyes.

Mr. Oglethorpe poured peroxide over the first wound and stuck the tweezers carefully into the hole, causing blood to run down my friend's chest. Ogie started to scream out in pain, but held back. I watched as Ogie's father performed makeshift surgery on his son in a manner even more primitive than what the room had seen a hundred years before. I wanted to turn away, but had to watch, even when the knife was used to make a hole larger so the birdshot could be retrieved. Ogie's skin sounded like paper tearing when the blade elongated the wound. I stumbled back and stopped myself from fainting by putting my hand against the wall and closing my eyes.

Peroxide and blood mixed in the seat of the rocking chair as Mr. Oglethorpe worked on his son like an old fisherman tying flies. The blood pooled and started to drip off the back of the seat creating a rhythmic tune of drops hitting the floor.

On the wall of Mr. Oglethorpe's office was a picture of him during Vietnam sitting in the pilot seat of a Huey Helicopter. All things military fascinate boys, and I was fascinated by the war that ended when I was three but had no memory of. My dad had lost friends and his first cousin in Vietnam and didn't talk about it.

Two of my uncles had killed men in Vietnam and, like my father, they didn't talk about the war. Too young to fully understand boundaries, I questioned Mr. Oglethorpe about the war like a reporter chasing a politician.

"Mr. Oglethorpe, is this picture from Vietnam?" I asked pointing at the black and white photo of the Huey.

"Yes, Augustus. That's from Vietnam."

"Why did you go to war? My dad said you could have avoided it because you were in college and your dad could pull strings."

Mr. Oglethorpe smiled, dug the tweezers into Ogie's chest and pulled out another piece of lead. "I could have gotten out of it, I guess. You're right. I could have, but I wanted to serve my country, so I dropped out of college and signed up."

"Are you glad you did that?" I asked.

"Glad? No I'm not glad. Proud maybe. Proud might be a good word. Son, Vietnam was a mess. Most of the boys didn't even know why they were there. I didn't feel it was right to send all the poor kids to war when those of us with a little more got off. It wasn't right." The elder Oglethorpe dropped the piece of lead into a glass cup that clinked when it hit the bottom. "Vietnam fucked up my generation. Even those that stayed behind got fucked up. Some went to college, some dodged the draft, but none really escaped that war. Everyone got fucked up."

"Yes, sir. I understand," I said honestly. This was the first time an adult had used the F-word with me directly. This was the first time an adult had ever talked to me like a man and from that time on I would relate the word "fuck" with man to man talks. It took a gunshot to get an adult to break the unwritten cussing law that prohibited adults from cussing in front of children and children from cussing in front of adults.

"Did it fuck everyone up because we lost?" I asked, emphasizing the word that was used in man-to-man conversations.

"Lost? An argument can be made that we won. I didn't lose, I'll tell you that. I killed a bunch of them and I came home. That means I won," he said as he poured more hydrogen peroxide on Ogie's wounds. "But it doesn't matter who won. None of the politics matter. Even if we had won, we would still be fucked up. Remember that son. Killing and war always fuck you up."

"Yes, sir. I will," I said. I remembered.

Now, the revelation of the identity of Ogie's girlfriend was a different kind of battle, but the fallout could fuck things, and people, up just as bad as war and we all knew it.

The pause was broken when Darwin said, "Your parents are going to kill you for dating a black girl."

"God, I know it…What, er, what do y'all think? What should I do?" Ogie looked at us with a confused face I'd never seen before. We turned our heads from Ogie to avoid eye contact because the look of confusion was like looking into the eyes of a man just convicted to hang.

Cassady said, "I don't know what to think, but I know you and you wouldn't do anything without thinking it through first. Not unless you were drunk, maybe, and even then you'd make a better decision than me." We laughed, then Ogie told us his love story as the rain began thumping the car roof like a drummer in time.

"Kendi's in my English class. Some of you know her—Kendi Johnson. She's different and I don't mean just because she's black. She's different than any girl I've ever met. Different from anyone I've ever met. She has those beautiful eyes. You know who I'm talking about?" We nodded that we did. "But it's not just her eyes. It's everything about her. She's got it all.

"We were assigned to work on an AP history paper together. First we met in the library to work together and then she had to come to my house to work late on a weekend. That's when it started…really started. I knew she liked me and I liked her too, but there was no way it would work so, I didn't do anything to encourage the feelings…in either of us. Then she kissed me—a real kiss right on the lips, tongue and all. I went with it and it felt good. It felt right. Not that I've kissed a lot of girls to know what to expect, but this one felt comfortable. That's the best way I can describe it, comfortable. Like it was meant to be."

Ogie fidgeted as he told us more of his escapades with Kendi. "Since then I've been meeting her in private. The first few times, I took her to the Majestic Lakes in the woods behind my house. I read to her. I guess that's cheesy, but I thought she would like it. I think she did. Then it really got hot, and, well…we've been doing it in the woods."

"Whoa man. What's that? You mean sex? Forest sex?" Darwin interjected.

"Yeah, you heard me, and in the woods. I told you I was doing it already anyway. Are you going to give me shit for it?"

"No, sorry. I forgot. I just never heard a story like this. I'm getting turned on. Please continue."

"Ok, well, like I said before I was interrupted. In the woods next to the lake. "Forest sex" as Darwin so eloquently put it. I'd prefer to say making love, we've been making love, and we've been doing it as often as we can. You know that neighborhood that's being built off Thigpen Road? That's where we've been going lately. I didn't want anyone to catch on to us at the lakes."

"Thigpen? Where you drop off your trash?" I joked.

Ogie cut my poorly timed joke short and continued his story. "No asshole. Not on Thigpen, the new neighborhood where we go to spin our tires. We have a plan where I pick her up at the high school and we drive out together. Then I park on one of the empty roads next to the woods. I leave a sign on my window that reads 'Out of gas – be back soon' just in case someone wonders why my car is there. I have a couple of blankets in my Dad's old Army duffle bag in my trunk. We make a pallet in the woods every night and do it while the owls watch us."

"You worried about getting caught?" Cassady asked.

"Yeah, a little, but that adds to the rush. I had a gut feeling we were going to get caught at the lake and that's why we went to Thigpen. But boys, I'll tell ya, there's still a rush doing it in the woods. I don't know what's going to happen, even though I really hope nothing happens."

"But, what if the wrong people catch you? Like her parents, or even worse some crazy ass rednecks?" asked Cassady. "She'd probably get hung from the nearest oak and you'd get your nuts cut off."

"Thanks for the thought Cassady. I don't think that's going to happen. When's the last time anyone got strung up around here?"

"My cousin knows someone in Heard County that hung a black boy," Cassady stated with confidence.

"Yeah, I'm sure he does." Ogie frowned. "The people I worry most about catching us are her two brothers. Y'all know her youngest brother from school. He plays football. Her older brother finished at Emory last year and is back at home until he finds a job. They're both big dudes and I wouldn't want to piss them off. But anyway, look y'all this isn't just a sex thing. I really like her. Maybe even love her…if that exists. I have looked at girls since I was ten years old. I've talked to a few hundred more and not one of them made me feel the way she does. In fact boys, most of them made me uncomfortable. I haven't related to one girl my entire life like I relate to her. She's different."

"Hell yeah she's different. She's black," exclaimed Cassady.

"That's not what I mean. I already told you. She's different from anyone I've ever known. Different from anyone I've ever touched. Do I need to go on? Because I can. I can spend the rest of the night explaining to you why she's special." We pulled into a dirt patch next to the bridge at Gethsemane Gardens. "Do me a favor y'all, and don't tell anyone. Not yet. My parents would kill me and I'd be chased out of town. My family's been here a long time. I don't know what this would do to the family name, but I bet it wouldn't be good."

"Screw your family name. When did family name become more important than love? Anyway, I want to hear more about the owls," I said

"Owls? What? Easy to say, Gus. Your family doesn't have a reputation to protect like mine," Ogie said looking down at his shirt like his surname was printed there. "But I think you're right. At some point I'm going to have to decide what's most important to me—my family or the girl I love."

I was irritated that Ogie said my family didn't have a reputation to uphold. No matter how much he hated class based on nothing more than birth, the concepts had been drilled into him and were hard to break. I knew this, and it still irritated me, but not enough to debate with him.

We left the car and walked through the after-rain fog, as the cold night air bit us like a nipping dog. Darwin said, "That's the most beautiful thing I've ever heard. It's like a Southern Romeo and Juliet."

When Ogie said his family had been in River Falls for a long time, he wasn't exaggerating. Though Ogie's real name was

Conrad Oglethorpe, in an effort to reject his legacy he preferred his nickname. It was almost as if it separated him from the rest of his family somehow. Ogie's family arrived in Savannah soon after Georgia's founding and they built stores selling supplies to newcomers and farmers. When the Indians were removed from west Georgia in the late 1820s and land was offered in lotteries, his family used the opportunity to become cotton farmers. They managed to get prime tracts of land with the lottery system working in their favor when a family friend "randomly" selected their tracts. The Oglethorpes' tilled thousands of acres of the newly acquired land for cotton, but the truth is that they did little of the labor; it was newly acquired slaves that did the work. When war broke out in the 1860s, his family fought to preserve their labor source and to protect Southern honor against Northern aggression. Ogie's great grandfather was a colonel in the Confederate Army and was instrumental in setting up hospitals in River Falls. He did this calculating that, if the Northern Army ever came near River Falls, the town would be spared and he was right. The smoke from Atlanta was in the air when General Sherman stopped in River Falls to visit injured Union soldiers. Sherman personally thanked Colonel Oglethrope before leaving orders to spare the area from destruction.

After the war, the family freed their slaves and, instead of dealing with sharecroppers, sold most of their land and built a cotton mill for the processing of textiles from farmers who held onto cotton and the sharecroppers who harvested the cotton— sharecroppers living in conditions not much better than slavery. As cotton farms moved from the South to other parts of the world, the Oglethorpe Cotton Mill continued to thrive because it didn't matter where the cotton came from. When materials came into vogue, the mill adapted and, by the 1980s, was processing various synthetics as well as cotton.

Ogie was expected to run the family business after college or, at the worst, become a doctor or lawyer. The Oglethorpes' ability to adapt kept the family prosperous through centuries, and Ogie had the tremendous burden of continuing the legacy and preserving the wealth for centuries to come. That same ability to adapt to changing times had lead Ogie straight into the arms of a girl that loved him, but it didn't fit into the image the family had created during those centuries past. He had few options and no matter what path he chose, there were no plans for a black wife in his future or a black girlfriend in his present. Kendi was beautiful, but she wasn't the blond-haired sorority girl most imagined him marrying someday.

Ogie resisted his elite status and preferred the company of anyone who didn't have blue blood running through their veins. I'm sure that's why he enjoyed our company. All four of us were from different backgrounds, but we all feared and resisted the norms of our world equally.

Chapter 4

"Welcome boys. Come here and give Mother Elly a hug. You boys are gettin' so big and tall," Mother Elly yelled to us as we entered the gates of Gethsemane Gardens. "Look what I just pulled outta the ground." Mother Elly was holding a pair of salad tongs that were gripped tightly around the tail of a black snake. The majority of the reptile's body was in a hole in the ground. "I woke him up. He was sleepin' through the winter. I got 'em though. Slippery little bugger." She laughed while pushing her long gray hair out of her face with her free hand.

"Mother Elly, what are you doing out here? At night no less?" I asked my great aunt.

"What's it look like? I'm catching sleeping snakes," she responded like I'd just asked a stupid question with an obvious answer.

Mother Elly was my father's aunt, and she was also a Hoodoo Priestess. Everyone in River Falls called her Mother Elly and she was known as the eccentric lady who drove around town in her red station wagon gathering items for her spells and potions. Elly, with her long gray hair and handmade hemp dresses, was even more famous locally than the old state governor that lived near River

Falls High School. She was famous in ways that embarrassed my parents and thrilled my friends. She was said to be rich, but my family knew nothing of any wealth. Many rumors persisted about her, but I'm not sure she minded. I think she might have even created a few of the stories. She was eccentric, but not crazy. Her dress, mannerisms and ideas on spirituality contrasted with everyone and everything in our conservative town, but it wasn't out of insanity, but choice. She had chosen her path early and had not strayed from it to please anyone but herself.

Elly had grown up on a small farm a few miles north of town. She was the daughter of a Scotch-Irish man and a Creek Indian woman. Her father was a devout Presbyterian and her mother a Native American worshipper of the earth, even though she kept this hidden from Elly's father. When Elly was 15, she married a traveling salesman from New Orleans who quickly moved her to Louisiana, a place where she knew no one. While there, she befriended by an old black woman who introduced Elly to Hoodoo and all its secrets. When Elly was 17, her husband returned from a sales trip and found bags of herbs, pieces of bones, human hair and books on Hoodoo. He was shocked and told her to stop practicing the craft or go home. She chose home, but not before her husband was tragically killed while chopping wood. Somehow the ax head broke free from the handle, bounced off a hard knot in the wood, ricochet back through the air and lodged itself between his eyes. Some say she made it happen with a spell, but as there was no law against using magic to kill, the New Orleans police simply forced her out of town and back to River Falls. I'm not sure if anyone thought to ask if she hit him with the ax and then broke the handle, but maybe they were so afraid of her they didn't even want her in their jail. I was told by my parents to never bring it up and even in my earliest childhood days I refrained from the subject.

After returning to River Falls, she lived in her old shotgun shack and performed psychic readings on Sundays. She was so popular that cars would line up for miles on the road leading to her house. When I was ten, a lady in a grocery store who knew I was Mother Elly's nephew told me the story of how she had helped her find a lost item. "Mother Elly told me the wallet was under the couch. She was right," the lady said.

I wasn't impressed and thought that "under the couch" was a pretty good guess. After that day, it seemed like Mother Elly started predicting one thing after another in my life that became true, or she knew things that no one else did. They were little things, but she always got them right. By the time I was a teenager, I had as much faith in Elly's predictions as the lady in the grocery store, but I didn't talk about my feelings as they didn't mix well at school or with my family. Despite my initial skepticism, many people believed in Mother Elly and she performed readings for years until her talents failed her. In 1980 she wasn't able to locate a lost child when a police sheriff asked her for help. The child was later found dead. She never offered her services to the public again for pay or pro bono.

"Mother Elly, can you tell us our fortunes today?" Cassady mocked.

"Oh, boy. Don't you get sassy with me. What do you fear? You don't think you believe, but you will boy. I tell you now you'll believe." She yanked the snake up from the ground, placed it in a pillow case and tied the opening shut so the snake couldn't escape. "I do feel something about you boys. You got good things to do, but right now you're just doing bad things. You've got to get your heads on straight and follow your hearts. There's just too much foolishness going on and it's gonna get worse." She turned to Ogie, grabbed his chin and pulled his face close to hers. "You can't fight love, boy. When it gets ya, it gets ya."

"Uh, yes ma'am." Ogie looked toward me, asking me without words to free him from her grip. I knew it was futile to resist her, so I watched as she moved closer to his face and sniffed each of his cheeks.

"Yeah, I'm right. You got love in you. Smell it a mile away."

Mother Elly released Ogie and grabbed Darwin by the arm as he started to turn to escape. "You smart and you know it. You just don't like to show it. Don't worry; you still got more learnin' to do. You got to get out there and feel life. You ain't gonna get all you schoolin in that big brick building. Some of it comes from getting knocked down. It's gonna hurt boy. It's gonna hurt bad."

"What, what are you talking about Mother Elly?" Darwin asked.

"Don't know yet boy. You'll find out soon enough I'm thinkin'. Yes you will." Mother Elly released Darwin, turned away from us and giggled as she walked into the shadows among the trees.

"What was that about?" Ogie asked when he was sure Mother Elly was too far in the woods to hear us.

I shrugged my shoulders. "I don't know. Just because she's my aunt doesn't mean I know what she's talking about. She's been coming up with odd stuff my entire life. But..." I stopped.

"But what?" Darwin asked.

I didn't want to continue because I knew the others would think I was lying. "But she's been right about too many things for me to discount her."

"Like what?" Cassady asked me. I could feel some heavy duty ridicule coming.

"Okay. When I was eleven, I broke my arm when I fell out of the oak tree behind my house. A few days before, she came over to the house and told me to stay out of the oak tree. I didn't know what she was talking about. I wasn't anywhere near the oak tree when she said it to me. I remembered her message when I was in the hospital getting x-rayed. I told my mother and she said it was nonsense, but then kept Elly away from me the rest of the summer. My mother thought Elly caused it, but I think she foresaw it."

"It was nonsense," Ogie stated with the confidence of a college professor. "Or it might have been self-fulfilling, meaning she caused it when she warned you about falling."

"She didn't warn me about falling; she said to stay away from the tree," I said, trying to preserve my argument.

"Whatever. She scared you and then your confidence was gone the next time you climbed the tree, even if you didn't think about it consciously." Ogie rebutted my argument.

"I guess you're right," I said, knowing there was little use debating with Ogie about something that couldn't be proven.

"Hey, should we stop her?" Darwin asked.

"Stop her from doing what?" I questioned.

"From taking snakes from the gardens. Our job is to protect this place. I think that includes the living creatures."

Cassady walked toward the trail, away from the direction Mother Elly had walked, and said, "If you boys want to tangle with that crazy bat go ahead, but I won't. She can have all the snakes she wants as far as I'm concerned."

"Then it is decided. The garden is safe for tonight and this meeting is closed."

I was lonely when I went home that night to an empty house. The quiet was broken only by the humming of the refrigerator and the buzzing of the streetlight outside that was flickering towards death. I had a postcard from my mother with an address in Denver that would be good for at least another week, so I wrote to my parents.

> Dear Family,
>
> Things are going well here in River Falls. I wish I could tell you that they built a bunch of new and fun things for us teenagers to do, but that would be lying. In fact, River Falls is the same boring place as ever. Well, not totally boring I guess. Ogie has a new girlfriend. He doesn't think his parents will like her, so he hasn't told them about her yet. She different, that's for sure. I still don't have a girlfriend and don't expect to have one any time soon. I think I need to gain some weight.
>
> I hope the tour is going well. I miss you all so much, but please don't worry about me. I'm old enough now and doing fine.
>
> Gus

Chapter 5

I figured it was a salesman when I opened the door, but instead found Elena. I stood and looked at her. I rarely did well talking to pretty girls, especially when I wasn't ready for them.

"You gonna invite me in or just stand there?"

"I'm going to invite you in," I said, but still stood in the doorway.

"Okay. I guess that means I can come in, but you're gonna have to move first."

I smiled and moved back so she could enter.

Elena was holding a brown paper bag with The La Siesta logo printed on the front. "My mother wanted me to bring you some food from the restaurant. She worries about you not eating enough."

"Wow, thank you." This was the first time anyone had brought me food since my parents had left with my brother to tour. "Do you want to eat with me? It looks like there's plenty of food in here." I looked into the bag. "Is that a bag of tortilla chips? I love those."

"Yes, those are chips, and no I don't want to share. If I never see another tortilla chip it will be too soon."

"Yeah, I guess you do spend a lot of time with Mexican food. Please come in, though. I could use the company."

Elena followed me to the kitchen, where I made us sweet teas and sat down at the table to consume the feast she had brought me. She sat across from me. "Do you miss your family? It's very lonely here," she asked.

"Sometimes." I stopped taking items out of the bag to think for a moment then said, "Mostly at night. Nights are the hardest, when it's quiet. It's not too bad most of the time."

"What about when you get sick?"

"My parents have insurance and I have a doctor to go to."

"No, I don't mean how you get better, but who takes care of you when you're sick? The best part about being sick is having my mother take care of me."

"I don't get sick often."

"You do sometimes though, don't you?" She asked.

"Yeah, I guess those times are tough. If I was really sick my mother would fly home."

Elena twisted her mouth to the left and looked at the table. "I guess that's okay. I need my parents around all the time. I love my family." She said she loved her family like I didn't love mine, but I hated arguing, so I changed the subject of the conversation to her.

"You have a great family," I said.

"Thanks. They have always been there for me. We're very close."

"That's a cultural thing I guess," I said wishing I hadn't as soon as the last word was out of my mouth.

Elena smiled and said, "Yes, People from South America love their families very much. Unlike families from Europe that hate each other."

"That's not what I meant," I said feeling my face burn hot.

"I know. I'm just trying to embarrass you. It's easy to embarrass you, so I like to do it often." She giggled and took a chip from the bag and ate it.

"I thought you hated those."

She shrugged her shoulders and crunched into the chip. "I don't know if it's cultural or not. I think we've just been through a lot together. I was five when we came to America. I learned English watching Sesame Street. Then I taught my parents how to speak English. I think it was easy for me, but they're still struggling. My papa won't let us speak Spanish at home. He insists we speak only English so that we'll all learn and be better."

"That makes sense," I said.

"Yeah, but it also makes for some tough conversations at home. When my mother gets mad she yells at my father in half Spanish and half English. One time he made the mistake of reminding her to speak English. She hit him with a lamp."

"Really?" I sat up straight. "Did it hurt him?"

"No more than he deserved," she said and giggled again before taking another chip.

I didn't want to know any more about her parent's fights, so I changed the conversation again. "Have you decided on any of the schools you were accepted to yet?"

"I will probably just go to West Georgia. It's close, so I can stay home."

"What! You mean you don't want to get away from all the tortilla chips you say you hate," I said as she took another chip from my plate. "Even though I get the feeling you don't hate them as much as you say."

"I'm happy here, Gus. I don't want to get out of town like you and the others. I like it here. This town took my family in when I was little and has been good to us. We have a church, a business and many friends. I know what I'm getting here and I like it."

"What if you meet someone that doesn't want to live here?"

"You mean someone to marry?" she asked.

"Yeah, marry."

"I haven't thought too much about it, but I will probably marry a local boy. If I meet someone else, he'll live here or it won't work out. There are a lot bigger things in life to screw up a marriage don't you think?"

"I don't know. I try not to think too much about things that far in the future," I said then smiled. "Sometimes I do maybe, but I try really hard not to. I can barely feed myself, much less figure out what kind of person I'm going to marry."

"I know you can't feed yourself. That's why you're so skinny. My mother thinks you are starving to death." She rolled her eyes.

"Will the guy you marry be Catholic?" I asked her.

"Maybe so, maybe not. He will have to go to church with me. It's important that we at least have the same beliefs. He doesn't have to convert, but I want him to believe in the same things I do—mostly anyway. I don't think God is a particular as the Catholic Church would like to believe."

"I think any guy would convert for you."

She blushed. "That's sweet, but they'd have to convert because it's in their heart, not just for me."

"I bet Darwin would convert for you." I mumbled the last few words knowing I had just told her about his secret crush.

"Darwin? Why do you say that?" She stopped and thought for a moment. "Oh... oh my... oh I see." She had been smiling, but was now solemn.

"I didn't mean to say that. I see that's not what you wanted to hear."

Her smile returned. "No, it's okay. I liked hearing it. I like him, but never thought... I mean...Darwin is so...he's so cool. I never even considered he would like me."

"He's not so unusual you know. He's really just a small town boy. He just dresses a little bit funny, but he's just a local guy. You know, a local guy just like you like," I suggested.

"Darwin." Elena said his name like she was learning a new word. "My mother likes him. He always talks to my dad when he comes into the restaurant and he's friends with my brother. He even tries to speak Spanish to my family sometimes, but it usually comes out all wrong. He's sweet, so we don't tell him. He's really sweet."

"You sound like you're sizing him up for marriage. I just slipped that he liked you."

She laughed. "I know. I know. I sound crazy. I do that with every guy I go out with. I size them up for marriage. I'm a dreamer, I think."

"It's okay to dream," I said. "So, what about Darwin?"

"I'll dream about it and we'll see," Elena said as she got up to leave.

Dear Daddy,

Things are going well here in River Falls. I'm not just saying that to make you feel better about taking off and leaving me here all on my own. That was a joke. I really am ok, mainly because of my friends. It seems they are making a point of looking after me. Or, at the least, they are keeping me busy, so I don't have much time to be lonely.

You know the family that owns the Mexican restaurant? Well, the daughter, Elena, brought me some chips today from her restaurant. Her mother thinks I'm starving to death. She doesn't know I'm just skinny—always have been. I took the free chips though. Darwin likes Elena, but she didn't know until I slipped up and told her. Did I mess up? Do you think he'll be mad at me?

I hope Dante is enjoying the tour. Let me know how things are going. I'm really enjoying all the postcards you keep sending. Tell mother not to worry. Tell her I'm fine. Gus

Chapter 6

"No way? You've never been to Rocky Horror? I can't believe it. My jaw's on the floor." Darwin opened his mouth, exaggerating it—his idea of a dropped jaw.

The group of us in the high school hallway shook our heads "no." Darwin had just told us the story of a midnight viewing of The Rocky Horror Picture Show, a very interactive movie that most of us hadn't even heard of yet. I thought the description of the film was ridiculous, but Darwin made the event around the film seem interesting.

"Well then, kids. I think it's about time you lost your virginity," Darwin responded.

"Darwin, how do you know I'm a virgin?" Yonah asked and then looked at me.

"Don't look at me. I don't know if she's a virgin or not." I could feel my ears burning as I looked down. Yonah liked to embarrass me and I really didn't know if she was a virgin.

"Okay, kids. Back to the movie. We're going," Darwin exclaimed.

Going to a midnight movie was out of the question for the others, Darwin being the exception as his parents were more lenient than others. My parents were in San Diego with my brother for a concert, so I knew I'd have no problem escaping for a night. Ogie, Cassady, Yonah and Elena would have to create a plan to escape curfew, so each told their parents that they were sleeping over at the other's house for the night. Words were carefully selected so as not to lie because each truly would be sleeping at another's house, but not until the next morning when we returned from the show. It was a simple plan that had worked in the past and would work again. We hoped.

The movie was playing at a mall theatre in the heart of Atlanta. Trips to Atlanta were rarely made by our families, and then usually to visit someone in the hospital or to pick up or drop someone off at the airport. To our parents, the city of Atlanta was a cesspool of violence, filth, and criminal activity. That's why our parents avoided it. To us, it was a cesspool of excitement, freedom and lawlessness. That's why we loved it. Occasionally, someone from Atlanta would transfer to our high school and, with them, they brought strange music and ideas as foreign to us as a South American tribesman. Venturing into the city was more than a trip to the movies. It was an adventure into a foreign and dangerous land.

We met at a motel near the theatre and parked near the room so we could see our cars through the window. Our mental pictures of hookers didn't match the real image of the drug addicted mothers that were far from sexy and not worth even the twenty dollar specials they offered us when we drove into the parking lot of the motel.

"Whatcha boys doing tonight? Ya wanna have a little fun? I'll throw in a deal for all a ya."

Chivalry was not dead, but decorum was so we rushed Yonah and Elena into the room as the sun set over the city.

"Y'all find the place okay?" Darwin asked as he stared at Elena's breasts held firmly in place by a black sweater.

"Barely. Thanks for springing for such a fine place," Elena responded.

"It was Cassady's doing. He's our travel agent for this cruise, ladies."

"Oh Cassady, honey. I think you might want to consider another line of work," Yonah joked.

Cassady smiled. "Like maybe a bartender. Here's the beer now."

A black man with droopy eyes and dry, gray hair stepped up to the motel window room and looked through the glass using his hand to break the mirror reflection caused by the setting sun. Cassady opened the door and the smell of booze, sweat and years of grime penetrated the doorway. The homeless man held two cases of beer under his arm.

"Thank you fine sir. You are a gentleman and a scholar," Cassady said before the homeless man sat the cases on the floor and held out his hand. "Oh yes. You need to be paid." Cassady opened a case of beer, handed the man two cans and then reached into his pocket and offered the man a ten dollar bill. "I hope this covers your trouble."

The homeless man didn't respond, but took the money quickly and put it in his right pocket. Then he took it out, held it up to the light and inspected the bill before moving it to his left pocket. He scanned the room and smiled an open mouth grin revealing four yellow teeth before stepping backwards toward the door.

Elena stepped toward him and grabbed his hand. "What's your name, mister? Do you have a place to sleep tonight?"

"My name is Willie. I sleep under the bridge. It's warm there."

Elena looked down at the beer and then back at the table where she had placed a bag of hamburgers. She walked over, removed two hamburgers and gave them to him. "It's nice to meet you Willie. My name is Elena. Thank you very much for the beer. You know, we're not going to be in this room after 11:30 tonight, if you want to sleep here."

Willie looked at Cassady, causing his cocky demeanor to break down. "Yeah Willie. You can have the room. I'll leave the key under the mat."

Later, the beer was gone and our alcohol buzz was humming when we left the room at 11:30 to find Willie standing at the door. "Guess I don't have to leave the key for you, do I Willie?" Cassady asked. "You enjoy the room and check out that shower. The girls even cleaned the toilet seat, so it should be nice and shiny. The bed is clean too. No one here even sat on it." Willie walked into the motel room and started picking cans from the pyramid we'd built to drink the remaining drops from each. I gagged and left the room for the car.

"I'm gonna do 'ole Willie a favor," Darwin said as he reached into his pocket. "Cassady, keep the car running." Darwin exited the car and ran over to a skinny black woman dressed in tight blue gym shorts and a red halter top. He handed her some money and pointed to the room we had just given to Willie. It was obvious what had just happened and I worried a cop was going to run around the corner and arrest Darwin.

"I can't believe you just solicited a hooker," I told Darwin as he climbed back into the car.

"Stop worrying, Gus. It's not like we're doing her. That would be illegal. We're minors and she's an adult, making it simply immoral."

"She's not for you?" Ogie asked.

"No man. She's a gift. A gift for Willie."

Yonah looked at Darwin and gently slapped the side of his head. "You're sick. I'm not even going to go into all the ways that was wrong." Her words caused Darwin's smile to retreat.

"He meant well," I said.

The Rocky Horror Picture Show was unlike anything any of us had ever experienced. It was a strange mix of stage show and audience assault that made us all want to run away, but kept us glued to our seats at the same time – like a car wreck that almost happened to us, but didn't.

"Do we have any more virgins in here?" A heavy man asked the audience. He asked again shaking drops of sweat from his face and head. "Do we have any more virgins? You better tell us or we'll find you."

"Answer him," Darwin whispered to us.

"Noooo." We all answered in unison. The truth was that we were all Rocky Horror virgins, but we didn't dare admit it. We had just witnessed what happens to virgins when the first group was taken to the front of the room and embarrassed as they were "sacrificed" on a fake alter.

Ogie scooted down in his seat and said, "I'm not saying shit. I'm keeping my seat the entire movie and I'm not getting up. Not to pee, not for anything. This is the craziest bunch of wackos I've ever seen."

"It's just a game, Ogie. Cool down. Nothing to worry about," Darwin said before patting Ogie on the head. "But if they come for us, I'm giving you up."

By the time we had been read the rules by the fat man, watched virgins sacrificed, had playing cards dropped on our heads, our hair soaked with water pistols and danced with some college girls in front of the theatre, I was thoroughly confused. Cassady yelled at the performers, who were dressed like characters from the movie, for the first half of the film, but fell asleep for the second half. When we left the theatre that night, he had toilet paper stuck to his shirt and rice falling out of his hair. He seemed confused by this, but so did I and I was awake for the entire show.

I tried to explain what the movie was about on Monday morning to a classmate and could only tell him it was about a sweet transvestite from Transsexual, Transylvania, but not the Transylvania in Europe—one in space.

Chapter 7

"If your gun jams, your ass is grass and the enemy's a lawnmower," Sergeant Dusty Raines said as he smashed a fist into his open left hand. He pulled his .45 caliber gun from the holster on his belt and pulled back the slide. "Soldiers, I want you to take a real good look at this weapon. It's clean. Clean as a newborn baby's ass. You won't find a cleaner weapon in this company."

Darwin raised his hand and started speaking before Sergeant Dusty could respond. "But, sir, isn't a baby's ass kinda dirty? You know with afterbirth and—"

Sergeant Dusty cut him off. "Don't call me 'sir.' I work for a livin'. And don't double talk me. I've seen Rambo I, II, and III and I can tell you that's as real as combat gets and unless you want to die, you better open your ears and shut your pie hole."

"Ok, um. Sir, I mean Sergeant. I understand why you would want your gun to be clean—" Dusty cut him off again.

"It's a weapon boy. You shoot with your dick? I don't think you understand anything."

"Ok, your weapon. I understand why you'd want it clean if we entered a real combat situation, but we are the Georgia Militia. We shouldn't be running into any firefights…should we?"

The militia sergeant shook his head. "Kids today. If you weren't the Captain's boy..." Dusty threw both of his hands in the air, walked away from us and lit a cigarette, ignoring the 'no smoking' signs posted on each wall of the junior high gym. He returned. "Private, you got a lot to learn, but I'm gonna teach you. You're right that we are not the first line of defense, but we are right behind the Georgia National Guard. That means if the regular Army gets taken out and then the National Guard gets knocked out we are the only defense left."

"Do we get guns...I mean weapons... if the Guard gets taken out, Sergeant?" I asked.

"Hell yeah, we get weapons. We get all the M-16s that are left. Good times."

Sgt. Dusty Raines was our platoon sergeant, and Darwin's father, Sherriff Mayflower, was the captain of the X-Ray Company of the Georgia State Militia. As Sherriff, he was able to easily establish a new company when the governor re-chartered the state militia that hadn't been in commission since the end of World War II and now was recommissioned in order to provide added security for fairs, political events and other functions where the police could use assistance. In fact, many of the volunteers for the militia were law enforcement officers. But there were also a few like Dusty Raines.

Raines never could enlist in the military as he'd never made it past junior high school and there was the little problem of a few drug arrests from the early 1980s. Now, Raines was the Sergeant over a platoon that consisted of Darwin, Ogie, and me. It was proper military etiquette to address a soldier by their rank and then their last name, but Dusty Raines insisted we call him by his first name because, "My Momma got around and there ain't no good way to know for sure if that's really even my last name." We just went with it.

"Uhhh ten chun." Sgt. Dusty snapped to attention like a diving board after a poorly performed dive and quickly saluted with his left hand. Darwin's father, Sherriff Mayflower – Captain Mayflower to us while drilling—walked into the room.

"He, he, he. Gentleman, how you doing? You enjoying drill today?"

We barked, "Yes sir."

"He, he, he. You know how to stand at attention. I see you've been teaching the men what they need to know, Sgt. Dusty."

"Sir, I have been teaching the men what they need to know to survive in case of an attack by foreign forces," Dusty responded.

"Foreign forces! What kind of foreign forces are going to invade Georgia? Alabamians?"

"Sir, well, I uh." Dusty stumbled over his words.

"Just teach the boys how to break up a fight, check IDs and run a riot line. And Dusty..."

"Yes, sir."

"Put that gun away. Ain't nobody going to hurt us. If the Russians come our way, you can get your gun out again." Mayflower grinned and walked from the gym.

Chapter 8

A couple of hours after our encounter with Sergeant Dusty, we were on the road again heading home. Or, we were supposed to be going home, but as young men do we wandered and soon found ourselves on the back roads of Caswell County. The exhaust from Darwin's 1970 Volkswagen van seeped into the cabin while we enjoyed the cold and silky darkness of the night.

The van had been Darwin's mother's. She had taken it to Woodstock and to San Francisco before returning to Georgia. After Darwin was born, she parked it behind her house where grass grew around the tires and tree sap covered the paint. At fifteen Darwin cleaned up the van, did odd jobs to pay for repairs and gave it a paint job that matched the Mystery Machine from the Scooby Doo cartoon.

"Oh man. Did you see that?" Darwin said as we zipped past an abandoned gas station.

"See what?" I asked.

"That sign. Did you see that sign?"

"Yeah, I guess. What's so important about it?"

"It's what it said, man. It said 'Mayflower Gas.' I gotta have that sign y'all," Darwin said to us.

Ogie was sitting in the back seat near the sliding door of the van. He reached over and opened it and then yelled over the sound of the wind, "Let's do it." The scene brought up visions a of Vietnam helicopter door gunner.

"I need some wall art and nobody's using it anyhow," Darwin said before slowing the van and turning around on the road. The van's headlights captured the eyes of a white-tail deer buck. His shoulder muscles flexed as we turned, but he didn't run or even walk away. Fearless. A chill ran up my spine. We returned to the abandoned gas station and Ogie jumped from the van, hit the ground, and rolled like a paratrooper. I followed, but my landing wasn't as graceful. When I hit the ground, I landed on an old piece of glass and cut my leg. The warm, sticky blood soaked my thigh and newly ripped pants. Darwin pulled the van behind the old building of the gas station.

I limped to the sign while holding my hand over the gash in my leg. Ogie was already pulling the old metal sign from the rotting wooden sign-post.

"It didn't look as big from the road," Darwin said.

"I need a crow bar or some sort of lever to get this thing off," Ogie said as he pulled and grunted.

"We have to hurry. I don't want somebody to see us," Darwin said as he wedged himself between Ogie and the sign. Ogie moved away and threw up his hands. Darwin put his right foot against the sign post, put both hands on one side of the sign and pushed with the strength of his entire body. The sign cracked free with a gunshot sound and Darwin fell back to the ground before quickly jumping back up.

"Oh shit. I cut my hand. My finger, I cut it. Damn that hurts," Darwin said as he walked in circles while holding his right hand with his left. "I'm bleeding everywhere."

"Yeah, me too," I said.

"Alright. Let's get out of here before someone gets killed. Can you get the sign, Ogie?" Darwin said as he pulled the shirt from under his winter coat and wrapped it around his hand.

I wrapped my leg in paper towels and tape that I found in the back of Darwin's van and stopped the bleeding, but Darwin wasn't so lucky. We spent the night at Darwin's house trying to get his hand to stop bleeding, but we found through trial and error that gauze, paper towels, duct tape and wads of toilet tissue were not enough, so Ogie and I brought him to the emergency room when sunlight broke.

"Find my insurance card, will ya, while I go to the back." Darwin handed us his wallet as he followed the nurse through double swinging doors.

"Look at this mess," Ogie declared as he opened Darwin's bulging brown leather wallet. "His wallet is full of junk. Here, help me get rid of everything he doesn't need." Ogie started pulling pieces of paper from the wallet. "Here's Yonah's phone number. Not sure why he has that. She doesn't put out, so toss it. Here's his class schedule. We can toss this too because if he doesn't know where to go by now it's too late. Get rid of these business cards. I don't even know who these people are."

"Dude, that's his stuff, "I said as I sorted through cards to find Darwin's insurance card. "And Yonah is our friend. Sex doesn't matter."

"Yeah, she's our friend that doesn't have sex with me."

"I don't have sex with you."

"Not my point, Gus. If I have to explain it to you, then…" Ogie's voice lowered as a gray-haired woman around 60 approached us.

"Hello, boys. My name is Ms. Grace. I volunteer and help friends and family members of those in need." Grace's calm voice made me feel like we were at my grandmother's house. "Can I get you boys anything? Would you like a Coca-Cola?"

We both said 'yes' and Grace left for a few moments before returning with two icy cups filled with the South's favorite carbonated beverage.

"You two look strong," Grace said as she touched my arm. "It's okay to be strong, but it's okay to be sad sometimes too."

Ogie's eyes widened as he looked at me before saying, "Thanks ma'am. We'll keep that in mind."

I stepped on his toe to keep him from insulting the kind old woman. Then I shook my head and looked at the floor to show Grace that I could feel sad. Well, at least I could appear sad.

"Do you boys need to call anyone? Where are the parents of your friend?"

"They are at work, ma'am. They told us to bring him on in and they would see him later," Ogie told her.

"Oh my. Don't they know how bad this is? He may not make it through the day."

With that, I stood up and responded to the shocking news. "What? What do you mean? He just cut his finger."

Grace looked back at the check in desk, but the hefty woman at the desk was helping someone else and couldn't verify whatever information Grace was seeking. "Are you boys not with the motorcycle accident victim?"

Dante,

I don't dare say dear to you in the greeting. You're my brother and that pretty much makes you my number one enemy in the world. I'm kidding of course, but only a little. I just got back from the emergency room with Darwin. He cut his hand last night after the militia meeting and it wouldn't stop bleeding. It was a total mess and the lady at the hospital got Ogie and me mixed up with someone else and started bringing us Cokes and stuff. It was pretty funny. I'll tell you more about it later because I don't think the story will be as funny on paper.

Listen, I'm glad you are doing so well. I am proud of you. I also miss you though, and I wish you all were home. I'm not trying to bring you down, so don't worry about me. I just needed to say 'I love you' even if you are my little brother.

Gus

Chapter 9

Everyone hung out at The La Siesta, but the restaurant always had plenty of empty seats thanks to the attached arcade and vast parking lot that were friendly to teenagers looking for places to loiter. With its large glass windows looking over Jefferson Street, just north of the court square, we could watch cars go by and laugh at our friends who got pulled over, almost daily, by the police. It was a game of cat and mouse and with several hundred high school students with cars and only a few officers the mice usually won on the back roads. But in town, the cats owned the streets and continued to pull over students in the same places.

Darwin pulled his Volkswagen van into the parking lot and I was reminded that Elena Luna's parents owned the restaurant when he said, "Elena's mother wants to see me. I've been dodging her for weeks. She always pinches my cheeks. Doesn't she know I'm not a little kid?"

"She's just calling it like she sees it," Cassady responded while looking out the window at a freshman girl that had successfully escaped her house for the night without her parents noticing her very short mini skirt and tight sweater. "You'll become a man when you get some of that."

"You're sick Cassady. She's just a freshman," Darwin said as he turned and saw the provocatively dressed underclassman. "But I could make an exception," Darwin mumbled as his eyes focused on the girl.

"Why does Elena's mother want to see you?" I asked, changing the subject because the girl and the conversation had simultaneously made me feel like a dirty old man at seventeen.

"Don't know. Maybe we can get some free chips and salsa out of the meeting, though."

"Free chips and Salsa, yes, yes my friends. That sounds like an excellent idea," Ogie said, stepping out of the van.

Señora Luna almost ran to Darwin when she saw us enter her restaurant. She grabbed both of his cheeks with her hands and then hugged him before pulling away while still holding onto his arms and said, "Hola, little man Darwin. You are growing so much." Her Argentinian accent covered her words like icing on a warm cake. "I have missed you. Why did you make me call for you?"

"I've been busy with school and stuff."

"Oh, that's no response to me. You little man. Come with me. I must talk to you."

Señora Luna took Darwin to a table in the corner of the restaurant, far from the arcade entrance, and prodded him into the chair like a mother directing her toddler. We watched with amusement as the Argentinian used her arms and body to emphasize her words.

Darwin smiled after she leaned over the table and whispered something to him. We tried to listen, but it was futile over the bubble gum pop playing loudly through speakers covered with sombreros. When it was clear we couldn't figure out the meaning of the conversation, we found a booth and sat down.

"So, what did she want? Does she want you to watch their dog again while they go on vacation?" I asked when Darwin met us at our booth a few minutes later. He was always their go-to guy to watch their family dog, Misty, when they left town.

"No, she doesn't want me to watch their dog again. She wants something much better. She wants me to take Elena to the Christmas dance at the Catholic Church next week."

"St. Mary's?" Cassady asked.

"No, the other Catholic church in River Falls." We all knew there was only one in our deeply protestant community and Darwin never missed a chance to point out a stupid question.

"That's great. So, are you gonna do it?" Ogie asked.

"Hell yeah. She's beautiful and I like her. She's one of the few girls I can even talk to without hurling."

"Really? From what I remember, you stumble over your words every time you talk to her," Cassady said before turning his head to look at a group of girls walking past our booth.

"Screw you, Cassady. It'll be fun, and I'm doing it for Señora Luna," Darwin said before we all laughed. "Okay, it's not for her really, but I would never be able to ask her out myself and now Señora Luna did it for me. The hardest part is over…I think."

I wondered what a Catholic dance was like. I had never been to a dance at a church. There wasn't much dancing in the Baptist church or by the Baptists even outside of the church walls.

Growing up Baptist and in the South, I had known only a few Catholics. While the rest of the world viewed Protestants as the wealthier of the two, my personal view was skewed by those few brave families that immigrated from the North that were almost always wealthier than all but the aristocracy.

Religion in the South was complex and I never really understood it. I'm not sure my parents did either, making it easy for them to stop attending when my brother's career grew into something too difficult to manage from the kitchen table. I was happy to have Sundays open when late Saturday night guitar concerts caused us to miss more and more church until we stopped going. People from my old church took our lack of attendance so personally, conversations with them in town or at school felt like those between two recently divorced, yet amicable, people.

"I'm glad for you, brother. Dancing in church sounds like a real blast," Cassady said as his smile twisted and his eye winked. "You go ahead and have fun at the dance and I'm going to get a little bit of that over there at that table."

"A little bit of what, Cassady?" I asked him. "Why did I ask that? I know." I rolled my eyes.

I turned to see Chastity scraping dried cheese from a table. She was probably the only American-born employee at The La Siesta.

I knew her well, at least as well as you can know someone that you talk to at the locker and make eyes with in the hallway. She was a sophomore at River Falls High and we had never had a class together, but we did seem to have some sort of connection, even if it was a relationship based purely on teenage sexual energy.

Cassady's intentions boiled my blood, not because I was interested in defending her honor, but because I was interested in her ruining mine. Chastity was almost as tall as me, with long blond hair and legs that seemed to stretch from her waist to infinity. Her body was tanned, even though it was December. Parts of my body longed to engage with her pouty mouth and pink tongue, but I couldn't decide which parts longed for her tongue the most.

"Boys, you better watch out for that little siren. She'll take you for a ride so fast, you'll lose your lunch," Ogie interjected.

"I hope so," Cassady said before catching her eye as she finished wiping the table. "Uh oh. She's coming over here. Be cool."

"Hey there, boys. Can I getcha anything?" There were so many ways to answer her question that was as creamy as Southern grown honey, but both Cassady and I refrained from saying what we wanted and she knew she had us both where she wanted us. "What are y'all doing for New Years Eve?"

"I, uh, well…" I tried to respond, but I had no plans and no good answer to a question so loaded.

"I bet we can think of something to do. What about you? You lookin' for something fun to bring in the new decade?" Cassady asked.

"Yeah, I gotta get out again. I've been in trouble for months. The only place I could go was work and school. The last few months have sucked."

"What did you get in trouble for?" Ogie asked not prepared for the response.

"I was screwing my boyfriend in my daddy's chicken house and my momma caught us. It was empty, you know. I wouldn't do that in there with all those chickens."

Darwin's eyes shifted up and then back down and Ogie's ears turned red. Cassady looked at me and covered his opened mouth with his hand. I sat very still, waiting for the rest of the story.

"We set up an old tent and put a bunch of blankets in it. It was real nice and real warm." She paused and squinted her eyes and tightened her nose. "But it did smell pretty bad."

"Who's your boyfriend?" I asked, trying to learn more.

"His name's Hank. You don't know him. He goes to East High, over in that other county you know. He's a football player. We don't go out no more though. He's too horny to go that long without a girlfriend."

Darwin straightened in his seat and said, "It's good to know he has his priorities in order."

"Yeah, I guess so." She responded without picking up on Darwin's sarcasm.

Cassady scooted toward the table and asked, "Well, what about you? Are you able to go that long with knockin' boots?"

"Hell no, son. I'm horny as a rabbit outta her cage. I ain't been laid in months."

As am I, I thought, after Chastity left to put in our order.

"Look guys. Y'all want to have a New Year's Eve party at my house? Nothing fancy. Just us and a few girls," Darwin asked.

"Yes, yes I do," Ogie said. "I want to have a party just to see Gus and Cassady fight over her. I can think of nothing else that would entertain me more on New Year's."

When Chastity returned, Cassady asked her to come to the party. I missed my chance.

"Oh yeah, I really want to come. I really do." Chastity's breast bounced when she jumped up and down after the invitation.

"Excellent. You can be my date," Cassady said winking at me. He had won that round.

Chapter 10

On Christmas afternoon, I spoke to Darwin about the dance he attended with Elena. He came over to my house to bring my parents and brother a gift from his mother, even though my family was away so my brother could play a Christmas concert in Washington D.C. Before he had a chance to talk to me, I knew he was different.

"Man, what's up with you? You're glowing. Are you pregnant?" I joked.

"I don't know what you're talking about. I'm not glowing, and I'm not pregnant."

"I believe you—at least that you're not pregnant, but something's up. Why are you so happy? Did you get laid?"

"Man, don't ask me that. We're talking about Elena here. She's a good girl. She's not like that and even if she was, her mother trusted her with me when she set the date up."

I felt my cheeks turning red with embarrassment. Darwin was falling for Elena, I knew it and had made a joke at his expense. "Sorry. I was just—"

Darwin cut me off. "It's okay. I know I'm the one that said there's no love, only lust, but I might have been wrong."

"Might have been?" I asked.

"She's as beautiful on the inside as she is physically. Have you ever known anyone that was beautiful on the inside, in their soul?" I nodded that I had, but I wasn't sure I understood it at the level he now did. "I don't know how to describe it, but she's the real thing. She's funny too."

"That's great man. I'm happy for you, I guess."

"You guess?"

"Well, I mean I don't know if I've ever known anyone to fall in love before. Not anyone in high school anyway. Real love anyway. Real love, like you're talking about."

"What are you talking about, Gus? People fall in love in high school all the time. I see it now that I know what it feels like. Look at Ogie and his new girl. That might be love. I guess we'll see. And look man, how many of our parents met in high school? That must have been real love because most of them are still together."

"That's because divorce around here means leaving town. You can't get divorced because you'll still see your ex-wife every day... and her family... and her friends, and her—"

Darwin cut me off again. "Yeah, I get it. What are we talking about anyway?"

"You, Elena, true love and something about internal beauty."

"Are you being a smart ass?"

"Maybe, but I don't mean to be."

"I know, it's natural." Darwin smiled at me. "She's coming to the New Year's Eve party at my house."

"You know how to end a relationship quickly don't you," I said.

"What do you mean by that?"

"Hanging out with Cassady, Ogie and me isn't the best way to prove to a girl that you love her," I responded.

"You're right, brother, but I figure if she still likes me after hanging out with all of us at once, I ought to keep her. Remember, she was at Rocky Horror with us. But I bought a hooker for a homeless guy. I wonder if that bothers her."

"Don't worry about that, brother. She'll like you. She may hate your friends, but she'll love you. If you can keep up with us, you can easily raise kids."

"What? Let's not go there yet. I don't think she's thinking that far ahead."

"I bet she is. My dad said girls start planning their weddings at about five years old. By the time they are in high school, they have everything planned. The only missing piece is the guy and as long as you look good in a tux you'll be fine. The next thing they figure out is what to name their kids. If your last name doesn't go well with their kid names you probably won't get past the second date. That's just a fact of life, Darwin. At least, that's what my dad says."

"You know, she does have pictures of her little cousins in her bedroom. Do you think she's already dreaming about kids?" I could see fear in Darwin's eyes when he asked me about Elena's young cousins.

"I don't want to scare you, but yes. And she's Catholic. She's going to have as many kids as God will give her. You better go to college and make a lot of money to pay for all those kids."

"I want to study English Literature."

"You're not going to make enough money teaching to pay for all those kids. You might want to consider medical school."

"I don't know. I don't think I like people enough to put up with all their whining," Darwin said.

"Then it's law school."

Chapter 11

"I read that the 90's are going to make the 60's look like the 50s," I said as we poured a large bag of ice into the sink to cover the beer.

"What does that mean?" Ogie asked me.

"I think it means the 1990s are going to be really wild and vulgar."

"You'll fit right in, Darwin," Cassady interjected.

"Tell me about it. I do love vulgarity, especially at the least appropriate times," Darwin said and then reached into the ice-filled sink and grabbed a beer. "Okay guys. My parents said it's okay to have beer tonight as long as we don't destroy the house. My dad's working tonight and mom is waiting for him at the station. I guess she's giving us our space. They will be home around 2:00 AM so we'll need to wrap this thing up and get the girls out before then." Darwin looked over his nose at each of us to confirm we understood the rules. "No problems?"

We agreed. "No problems."

"Good. Who's going to make it? What girls are coming?"

Ogie cleared his throat. "Kendi is coming, Elena and Yonah. Of course, Chastity is coming too."

"Uh hum. Did you say Kendi? You finally coming out of the closet with her?" Cassady asked before taking a drink from a bottle of rotgut vodka.

Ogie shrugged his shoulders and seemed to shrink in size before answering in a meek voice, "Yeah, y'all cool with that? We can't keep meeting in the woods forever, you know."

"No, man. That's cool. I'm proud of you. Good man, Ogie," Darwin said before giving Ogie a hug and then pulling Cassady and me into the group.

"Okay, dude. You can let me go now," Cassady said before continuing, "This is way too gay for me." He looked up toward the ceiling in prayer. "God, please make the girls hurry. I don't want to pass out around these three."

At 8:00 PM, we saw Elena's car from the window in the kitchen door. She was alone. We had expected Yonah to come with her, but she had decided to stay with her mother for New Year's Eve. Few expected Yonah's mother to make it another year, even though no one voiced this opinion, especially to Yonah. Before Darwin could open the door for Elena, another car pulled into the gravel driveway. It was Chastity.

"Who's ready to party?" Chastity yelled from the rolled down window of her faded yellow Datsun. "I know I am! Woo hoo!"

Cassady put his hand on my shoulder and quietly said, "I love her name—Chastity. It's like an invitation. It's like a challenge."

"That's just really great, man. Why do you think she wants you anyway?" I asked.

"What makes you think she doesn't?"

"Oh, I don't know. Maybe because you're obnoxious. Maybe because you only want to do her. Maybe because she's just a challenge to you, a game."

"What's so wrong with that? You heard her story about doing her ex-boyfriend in the chicken house. She's easy. She wants the same thing I want. What do you want from her?" Cassady asked.

"Yeah, I want her too. Just like you do, but I might be interested in getting to know her first and maybe, just maybe, having a relationship with her. Won't know until I get to know her first, though." I heard the hypocrisy in my voice. Part of me believed my words, but another part knew I was jealous.

"Are you kidding me, dude? What's with the Boy Scout persona?"

"I don't know," I said, feeling embarrassed because I had just crossed a line in the guy code. "We'll just have to see who she likes the most. You might be Mr. Confident, but I have a few tricks myself. I'm sorta funny you know. Girls like funny…don't they?"

Chastity wore a pair of acid-washed jeans so tight they looked like they had been applied with spray paint. She wore a denim jacket and a tight button-up white blouse that accentuated her large, round breasts. She walked up to me and kissed me on the lips. This was surely a sign that she was interested in me and not Cassady, but before I could make eye contact with Cassady to gloat, she kissed him too. Then she put her arms around Elena and hugged her. I was hoping she would kiss Elena, but it didn't happen. Life is so unfair.

"So who wants to get drunk?" Chastity asked before taking Cassady's vodka and putting it to her lips. She leaned her head back and drank so fast air bubbles gurgled to the top. She shook her head and said, "Hell yeah, boys! That's what a girl needs!"

Elena pursed her lips and raised her eyebrows before grabbing Darwin's hand and leading him to the large living room. We all followed, leaving the door open despite the chill of the forty-degree night air. Chastity now had the vodka, so Cassady carried several beers from the sink with him. He handed me one and I sat on the long leather couch next to Darwin and Elena. I was hoping Chastity would sit next to me, but instead she walked over to the stereo under the TV and turned the radio to a station playing top-forty popular music.

Chastity stepped onto the coffee table and began moving like an exotic dancer, changing the way I would hear the Debbie Gibson song forever. She looked at me, moved side to side and slowly slid her coat from her shoulders before letting it fall to the floor. I hadn't noticed her red high heels before, but I did now as she lifted one foot and slid it down her leg. Her fingernails were painted bright red and she took her index finger and put it in her mouth before tracing a line down the center of her chest to her crotch. Without her coat, I again noticed her large and round breasts bubbling under her shirt. She noticed where my eyes landed and answered by unbuttoning the top button of her shirt. A hint of her white lacy bra caught my eye like a diamond on the ground—a diamond I wanted to examine more closely.

She lifted the vodka bottle and poured it into her mouth, with most of the liquid running down her neck and soaking her shirt and bra. My blood pumped hard through my body while her hips swayed. Tunnel vision grew around her like she and I were the only people in the room. I knew she would be mine. Then the door knocked and the trance was broken. I heard Kendi's voice.

"Who left the door open? Don't you people know it's freezing outside?"

"Kendi's here," Ogie said standing quickly and walking into the kitchen to meet his girlfriend. The dance was over, but everyone remained quiet as we tried to listen to Ogie and Kendi. Their voices were hard to decipher over the loud music from the radio.

"Hey, speak up will ya?" Cassady yelled while leaning back over his chair and looking into the kitchen. "Whatcha doin' in there? You ain't making babies are ya?"

"Shut up Cass," Ogie quickly responded.

"Fine, fine. I'm just messing with you."

I don't know if it had ever occurred to Chastity that whites and blacks could find each other interesting because she stepped off the table and sat next to me when Ogie and Kendi came into the room holding hands. Chastity leaned over to me and stated the obvious. "Ogie's got a black girl with him."

"Yes Chastity, he does," I said hoping Kendi hadn't heard her.

"I just don't get it."

"Please be quiet," I said as I put my hand on her knee and pushed down like her leg was a volume knob.

"Everyone, I'd like to introduce Kendi. I think most of you know her from school." Ogie introduced his girlfriend and everyone smiled except for Chastity, who sat on the couch looking at her coat on the floor. Ogie was never one to miss a moment to debate with or embarrass anyone who didn't match his wit and jumped on this opportunity. "Chastity, I see you're thinking hard about your coat. Don't worry; it seems to be all denim. I don't believe any animals were harmed in the making of your coat."

"Huh?" Chastity looked up at Ogie like she had just woken from a coma.

"Your coat, Chastity. I believe it is animal-free."

"Yeah, I…uh. You have a black girl with you."

"That's right Chastity. It's your insight and knack for the obvious that impresses me most. Of course, my friends are interested in your other attributes."

"What?" Chastity remained confused.

The moment was deteriorating, so Darwin interjected. "Okay, all. I think it's time we get a snack. Elena has been kind enough to bring chips and salsa from her parent's restaurant."

"Yeah baby," I said, jumping from the couch and using this as an opportunity to follow Darwin's lead to break the tension. "Those chips are so good."

Ogie's hand fed Kendi a chip piled with cilantro rich salsa. She smiled and looked into his eyes while I looked into hers trying to find some notice of anger or pain due to Chastity. But instead, I only noticed affection for Ogie.

I was no master of women's emotions, but I knew enough about life to see real appreciation for another person and maybe even love. I had never seen Ogie so visibly happy, but I'd never seen him with a girlfriend either. Not for any real time anyway. He did take a girl to a dance in tenth grade. They hung out for a few weeks before the dance; at the dance, she told him she made a mistake and wished she had gone with someone else. She left him during the dance and started making out with Chuck the Greaser. Chuck always hung out in the auto shop at school, but never seemed to be working on the cars much. He hung outside the doors of the building and smoked a lot. He was the only kid in school that was allowed to smoke on campus. Some thought it was because he was 18, but I think the reality is that the administration just hoped that if they ignored him, he might graduate or wander off like an unfed stray dog. Ogie learned then that being nice didn't get you the girls. Not teenage girls, anyway, that were genetically linked to bad boys that probably were better mates thousands of years before, but thanks to evolution of society, they had little to offer in an educated world that rarely needed protection from invaders and tigers. But most of the teenage girls we knew made a strong argument that they had not evolved every time they chased another guy we labeled as a "loser." Our pain came every time another "loser" got the girl, and academic achievements and science awards were no substitute for the love of a woman.

Now Ogie had a girl that valued him for all the right reasons. I couldn't help but condemn Chastity's ignorance, but the truth was that I hadn't seen too many whites and blacks in relationships either. We all had black friends in school, but I couldn't remember one time when I had gone to a black friend's house as a kid. We didn't mix in birthday parties; we didn't go to the same churches. There was no obvious racial tension in River Falls that I could see, but due to a million things that happened before I was born, there were two worlds. I had never even thought about it until Ogie and Kendi. Now they were busting that world wide open, rewiring my mind and I was surprised that I didn't care. Just like Darwin had said, they were Romeo and Juliet. Their love was more beautiful than all the hate that surrounded them.

"Listen, man. There's three chicks here tonight. Two are taken. That means we have to either share Chastity or figure out who's gonna get her," Cassady said to me and winked.

"Are you kidding me? I'm not sharing with you. And share her? That's the grossest thing I've ever heard," I said, and thought a minute for a better response that didn't come.

"What? Are you afraid of seeing me naked?" Cassady asked before grabbing his crotch. I actually had to think about it before responding that nothing was worth seeing him naked. I wasn't ready for anything that kinky. I had no illusions of losing my virginity in flower-covered fields or Victorian bedrooms like the girls at the party, but my vision definitely didn't include Cassady.

"Well...yes I am. I can't think of a single thing in this world that scares me more."

"Even if it gets you laid?"

"Uh, yes. Even if it gets me laid, because getting laid at the same time as you and with the same girl just doesn't sound like much fun."

"Okay, but I'm going for her man."

"Really, you would do that?" I asked.

"Yes I would, and I am. I've already started working her over," Cassady said before poking a hole in the bottom of a beer can with his pocket knife, turning the can upside down to his mouth and then opening it so the entire beer rushed into his mouth.

Four hours later, the alcohol had done its job of turning obnoxious, sex crazed teenagers into raging, dangerous, destructive and obnoxious, sex crazed teenagers. For at least two of those four hours, Ogie and Kendi made love in the bed of Darwin's parents, but now were in the kitchen making scrambled eggs, an obvious thing to do after having two hours of sex; Cassady had dented several aluminum trash cans with his head; the cats had disappeared through the open kitchen door; Darwin and Elena were sitting on the couch zoning to one of Mrs. Mayflower's Miles Davis' records. It was now a few minutes until midnight and the beginning of a new year, the beginning of a new decade, and I was coming down from my high. A feeling of defeat had come over me as I realized my battle for Chastity was lost. She was in Darwin's room and the door was closed. In my mind, I knew what was about to happen or what was already happening and it ate at me like a rat eating through a box of food.

"Why the sad face?" Kendi asked me as she sat down next to me with a plate of eggs.

I didn't want to tell her why I was sad, but I was still drunk enough to overcome my inhibitions and said, "I really liked Chastity. Thought I did, anyway."

"Oh, I see, and Cassady is with her now?"

"Yeah, they're in Darwin's room doing God knows what."

"I'm sure God does know what they're doing," Kendi said and smiled.

I forced a smile in return.

"Gus, there are other girls. Girls that are a lot better than her. She's not right for you. Do you want to marry a girl like that?

"Who said anything about getting married? I don't want to marry her, but I sure would like to date her," I said. "At least for a few weeks anyway."

"You and every guy in school," Kendi said sitting back and lifting the fork to her mouth. "If you want her, go get her."

"Yeah right. It's not that easy. I've already tried."

"No, I mean it, and it don't look to me like you tried all that hard," she said before swallowing a mouthful with a gulp. "If you want that dumb brick, go in there and take her from Cassady. Ain't no reason he should have her if you really like her. She might be interested in something real. That's probably all she's looking for, anyway. She just doesn't know how to go about getting it, so she does what she does. I'm guessing what she really wants is someone to make her happy. I'll bet something is missing in her life. Or…or maybe she just likes sex. You won't know, though, unless you try," Kendi said as she pushed herself from the couch. Before walking away, she turned and said, "If you want her let her know."

"Yeah, I will," I said.

With new found courage, I stood up and went to Darwin's bedroom. The door was locked, so I knocked. No answer. I knocked again, this time louder.

"What? Go away," Cassady yelled from beyond the door.

"I want to talk to Chastity."

"No, go away."

"I'm not going away. Let me talk to her for a minute and if she wants to go back in there with you after we talk, she can."

Cassady responded louder and his words were broken when he said, "What the hell, man? Can't you take a hint? Now get out of here."

I took a deep breath and started to turn before regaining my courage again. I knocked harder and yelled through the door, "I can't take a hint and I'm not going away. I want to talk to Chastity."

"Are you fucking kidding me?" I heard Cassady grumble. "If you want in, you'll have to kick the door in because we're in bed."

"Ok, then. Why the hell not?" I said before kicking the center of the door as hard as I could, splitting the door in two creating a popping sound like a small gun firing. The split of the door revealed the two in bed together, close and under the sheets. Cassady was hand-feeding a donut to his newly captured mate. Chastity was startled when she realized what had happened, but

Cassady sat still holding the donut to her mouth. He looked at me, but kept his hand in place.

I didn't care that I had just destroyed Darwin's door or that his parents would be incensed when they saw it. I only felt jealousy and the rage that accompanies jealousy—rage heightened by alcohol and in that rage, I said what would end their tryst and possibly my friendship with Cassady.

"I don't care how many donuts you feed her, she's not going to fuck you," I shouted.

The busting of the door didn't get her out of bed, but this did. Cassady looked at her as she crawled from the covers and pulled her jeans over her red underwear. I finally saw her bare chest when she moved her hands to put on her shirt, but I felt guilty about the way her breasts were revealed to me. With the realization that I had just ended his New Year's fling, he gazed at me, tightened the skin around his eyes and focused them on me like a riflescope.

"You stupid boy. Look what you've done," Cassady yelled at me as he jumped from the bed to face me.

"What, you don't want to share? Did I keep you from completing the challenge? Did I keep you from getting some of that white trash ass?"

"You better get the hell out of my way, you son of a bitch," Chastity said while pushing me with all her weight.

"No problem," I said as I grabbed the edge of the doorframe to steady myself while moving to the side to let her leave the room.

Cassady's face was turning as red as a sunburned kid on the beach. He ran out of the room and grabbed Chastity's arm, but she pulled away and went through the kitchen to her car. The house door slammed shut at the same time Cassady walked up to me and looked me in the eyes. I stood my ground and watched for his body to move, anticipating a punch. I wasn't going to hit him first, but if he moved toward me, I was ready to defend. What was only seconds felt like minutes as the only sound was Dick Clark on the TV. With our eyes locked, we heard the countdown to the New Year. It was a new decade. It was 1990.

Chapter 12

A scream woke me from my drunken stupor. I sat up and noticed Cassady sitting next to me. I had fallen asleep in the guest bedroom bed after the fight; Cassady must have come in sometime after. We heard another scream. It was Darwin's mother.

"What should we do?" he asked, as we heard Mrs. Mayflower stomping through the house and screaming at each discovery of the party damage.

"I don't know. I'm not leaving this room," I said.

"Me either. Do you think we can get out the window?"

"Don't know. Let's see," I said and got out of the bed and went to the window. I tried to open it, but it was sealed with paint. "It won't open. It's painted shut."

"Bust it. Knock the glass out. We can't stay here," Cassady said. I looked at his face to see if he was joking; he was not. I shook my head no.

Cassady moved to the edge of the bed and reached down for his shoes. He put them on and went to the door. "I can hear her walking around. She's pissed. I think she might kill us." Mrs. Mayflower screamed again. "Oh yeah, she's going to kill us. Gus, you have to break the window. It's us or the window."

"I'm not breaking the window. Let's just be cool. Maybe she'll leave."

"Or maybe if we wait long enough, she'll die of old age. Gus, break the window."

"No Cassady, I'm not breaking the window. She's already mad enough. What's going to stop her from shooting at us as we run from the house?"

"Good point. Let's just be very still and hope she doesn't come for us."

The screaming stopped and we both sat on the bed. We didn't move, we just looked at each other. Darwin and Ogie were talking to Mrs. Mayflower, but we couldn't understand what they were saying. After 20 minutes, Darwin knocked on the door. "Guys, my mother wants to talk to you," he said through the locked door. We didn't answer. "I know you're in there." Then he whispered, "Come out before she gets mad again. My dad has her calm..."

I unlocked and opened the door and we followed Darwin to the kitchen where Sheriff Mayflower and his angry wife sat at the table. Millie Mayflower was not the thin girl she was when she met the then deputy Mayflower at a war protest in the 1960s. The years had added more than a few pounds and now Mrs. Mayflower was the type of lady that made people say, "If she were thin, she sure would be pretty." Despite the years, the sheriff loved every pound of her and always made her feel beautiful, but on that night her beauty was masked by anger.

Sheriff Mayflower looked up at us and laughed. "He, he, he. If it ain't Captain Vodka and Super Six Pack."

I leaned over to Darwin and asked, "What's he talking about."

"Just shut up and listen," Darwin responded.

Mrs. Mayflower wasn't smiling and looked at her husband and said, "This isn't funny. These boys are underage and you're the Sheriff. What if people found out about this? Do you know what would happen if one of them got hurt last night?"

"A little beer never hurt nobody, honey," Sheriff Mayflower said.

"A little beer has hurt plenty and it's not just beer. There's liquor too. What if someone with the newspaper found out about this? What if one of these boys died?" She said before standing up and pouring the rest of a bottle of vodka down the sink. Cassady reached out to save the vodka before I put my hand up and stopped him. He looked at me and I was sure I saw a tear in his eye.

"Mom, I thought it was alright to have a little fun since it was New Year's Eve and all," Darwin said.

"You can have fun, but you don't need to get drunk to do it." She dropped the empty vodka bottle in the trash. "You didn't have girls here did you?"

"No ma'am. No girls at all," Darwin stated affirmatively. We all nodded.

"Really?" Mrs. Mayflower asked before opening the knife drawer and pulling out a white bra. "Then who owns this? I found it in Darwin's bedroom…next to the broken door."

"Ma'am, that would be Gus. He thought it would be funny," Ogie said trying to come up with a quick answer.

"You're lying, Mr. Oglethorpe. And if you're not lying, you boys have some explaining to do to your parents."

Darwin said, "We did have girls here. They left right after midnight."

"So you let drunk girls leave my house?" Mrs. Mayflower asked.

Sheriff Mayflower looked at the table and started drawing lines with his finger. He had just bowed out as our defense. We were on our own now and we knew it. Cassady saw this as a chance to get me back for ruining his shot with Chastity and offered an explanation in his best adult manner.

"Mrs. Mayflower, if I may. I took the nice young lady to Darwin's room to talk and Gus became confused as to my intentions and…"

Mrs. Mayflower interrupted. "To talk? You're bullshitting me Cassady. I know better than that."

"Yeah, this lady knows bullshit. I haven't been able to get one by her in years," the sheriff said, making everyone laugh but his wife.

Mrs. Mayflower threw up her hands, seeing that she wasn't getting any help from her husband. She looked down at the bra and threw it into her husband's lap. "Enjoy this. It's all you'll be getting for a while." The sheriff sniffed the bra as Mrs. Mayflower stomped to her room. We heard her scream again. "Who's been in my bed? Who's been messing around in my bed?"

"Don't feel bad boys. I'm not getting any anyway," the sheriff said before handing the bra to Cassady and walking to the door that lead outside.

"Really, Sheriff? But you're married. Don't you have a lot of sex when you're married?" Cassady asked honestly.

The sheriff laughed. "Not as much as I'd like, but there's still fun things you can do as a married couple."

"I don't want to hear this, dad," Darwin said. "This night has been confusing enough and I really don't want to hear this."

"Don't worry, son. It's not what you think." The sheriff moved from the door to the refrigerator and opened the freezer door. "You boys see all that ice cream? How much do you think is in there? Looks like five, six gallons of ice cream."

"Okay, dad. I really don't want to hear about this. This is just too much."

"Get your head out of the gutter, son." Sheriff Mayflower took out a gallon of ice cream and a spoon from a drawer and scooped a mound of vanilla ice cream before continuing. "Just because a man doesn't have a lot of sex doesn't mean he can't have a little fun. I keep this freezer stocked with ice cream. Darwin's mamma got pretty heavy the last few years. A few months ago, I noticed that no matter how much ice cream I bought she always ate it within a couple of days. Since then, I've been buying ice cream every day. I'm seeing how long it takes her to eat her weight in ice cream."

"Dad, I don't know how to respond to that," Darwin said.

The sheriff smiled and put his hand on Darwin's head. "There's a moral to this story boys. You have to keep a marriage interesting for it to last any way you can." With that, the sheriff went outside and carried his ice cream into the darkness. He left the door open and the chill of the January night hit us like a wall of ice.

I was now sober and the cold woke me even more. I realized I had ruined Cassady's night and had done so after my chances were long over. I had to apologize.

"Man, I'm sorry about what I did," I said to my friend.

"Yeah, dude. You were a prick. I offered to share her with you."

I shook my head and said, "Yeah, I know you did, but that wasn't going to happen. I have no intention of sharing my first time with you. There's a lot of things I like doing with you, but a ménage á trois isn't one of them."

"I didn't take Spanish so I don't know what you just said, but if you're apologizing, I accept."

"That's what I'm doing. I'm sorry. I won't cock block you again."

Ogie grabbed both of us by the neck with his big hands and squeezed. It hurt, but I didn't struggle, figuring it was my punishment. "Let's make an agreement right now that we'll never let a girl come between any of us again. We are friends and from now on we support each other in all things, including love. Never again will we fight over a girl."

Darwin completed the circle by placing his hands on our shoulders. "I agree."

We all agreed.

Daddy,

I'm learning a lot about human nature. You once told me nothing good ever happens after midnight. I agree with you now. I was at a New Year's Eve party and stayed overnight. That's when I almost got into a fight with Cassady. It won't happen again. I think we both learned from it, but that doesn't make it feel any better. It's so easy to say or do the wrong thing and hurt someone.

Speaking of hurting others, I'm learning a lot about blacks and whites and how we interact and think about each other. I guess I never thought much about it before. Things just were the way they were. That really doesn't make sense now. I'll tell you why later.

I miss you all so much. I wish you were home, but I understand Dante's career may not get another shot. Hug everyone for me.

Gus

Chapter 13

"Jocks are messing with Sean," Cassady said as he approached us outside of the school.

"Okay, well, good morning to you too," I responded.

"Yeah, good morning. Look, he's too little to defend himself," Cassady noted and looked at each of us, asking with his eyes for our help. "We're the S.S.D. It's our job to protect those that can't protect themselves and Sean is our friend."

"I wouldn't say he's our friend," Ogie said. "And Sean probably asked for it. You know how he talks too much."

"I'm with Ogie on this one and I hardly know the guy anyway," I said.

Ogie was right about Sean talking too much. Sean McDillian had angered more than a few people, but not enough to drive them to violence.

Sean was barely five feet tall and my experience had taught me that short guys usually had a Napoleon complex that they covered either with humor or by fighting. Sean tried to be funny, but often fell short and simply pissed off the target of his jokes. Unfortunately for him, he didn't like or know how to fight and often ended up apologizing.

"Sean's just a little sophomore. The jocks messing with him are seniors. If we don't do something they'll beat the snot out of him," Cassady said trying to sell the defense of Sean.

"Fine. I'm in—for you Cass. Not for him. Where do I need to be?" Ogie asked.

"Thanks, man. I knew you'd come through. We're going to watch him from a distance when he walks home today after school." Cassady looked at Darwin and me. "What about you two? Are you going to let Ogie do all the dirty work?"

"Ogie can handle a few jocks by himself," Darwin said and looked at his watch.

"Maybe he can, but what if one of them jumps him? Who's going to watch his back? Maybe you don't care what happens to Sean, but I know you care about Ogie. Anyway, we are the S.S.D. Don't you remember?"

"Okay, okay. I'm in too, but I'm not fighting anyone. My dad would ground me till graduation if he caught me fighting."

"What about you? Three against one isn't fair. We need to show them what it's like to be outnumbered." Cassady looked at me and folded his arms.

"I'm in," I said reluctantly.

I had forgotten about my agreement to follow Sean home until I went to the parking lot after school and found Cassady, Darwin, and Ogie leaning against my Mustang. Their faces were cold as the dark January sky. They were mentally ready for combat, but I was not and knew I had to change my mindset quickly.

"Hello, guys. I guess we're doing this?"

"Hell yeah, we're doing this." Cassady pushed away from my car and stood straight. "Sean asked me to not follow him, so we have to stay way back. He lives on Bailey Drive, so he should pass by the parking lot on his way out."

Ogie nodded toward the backdoor of the high school gym. "See the jocks? They're standing between the bushes and the gym door. We think they're waiting on Sean. What they don't know is that we're waiting on them."

"We've secretly replaced their fine bullying with an unexpected ass-kicking," Cassady joked, copying a popular coffee commercial.

We all laughed, but our laughter didn't hide the nervousness.

We fidgeted at my car until we saw Sean leave the math building and walk toward Lagrange Street on his way home. He didn't notice the jocks behind the gym and the jocks didn't see us follow them when they walked to Lagrange Street behind Sean. The streets around the school were busy with students and teachers and no one seemed to notice anything unusual.

Sean crossed the last road before his street and was immediately pushed off the sidewalk by a rushing jock. Sean hit the ground hard and tried to stand up when the next jock punched him across the jaw. Sean curled into the fetal position and the third jock spit on him.

"Hey, boys. I think you better leave him alone," Cassady yelled as he ran toward the beating. "You better leave him alone or I'm going to –"

Cassady was cut off when the first jock kicked Sean in the ribs. "Or you're gonna do what, Cassady? You fucking turd."

Cassady reached the brawl before the rest of us and immediately jumped toward the largest of the jocks, but was deflected, hit the dirt hard and rolled back into the road. The next jock tried to kick Cassady but he rolled farther into the road and jumped back up to his feet. The three were busy with Cassady and didn't notice Ogie, who was running at full speed and hit all three boys, knocking them to the ground. This was a hit that would end most fights but the jocks had spent years getting hit in football practice and recovered quickly to jump on Ogie, who had knocked the air out of his lungs in the assault.

I reached the fight and deflected pushes and kicks with my back while pulling Ogie from the tornado of feet and hands. I tried to stand, but was hit in the back with a rock one of the jocks had found nearby. I rolled away to some bushes and tried to catch my breath which felt like it would never return. I expected another hit, but it didn't come. I looked up to see Darwin hit the first jock with a short metal rod knocking the jock out. The second jock was lying on the ground holding his bleeding head. I would learn later that Darwin had popped him with the rod, right after he hit me with the rock. The third jumped on Darwin's back, but Cassady pulled him off by his hair and then hit him in the face so hard it sent that jock to the ground as well. All three bullies were lying on the ground. One was motionless, while another crawled in circles and grunted in pain. The first jock was knocked out, but Darwin's anger didn't subside and he raised the rod in the air and resumed the assault with blows to the football player's midsection.

"He's down, Darwin. He's down. You can stop," Cassady yelled at Darwin to stop his barrage of blows on the body of the broken jock. "Darwin stop... stop!" Cassady reached around Darwin's body from the back and pinned his arms to his side. Darwin squirmed like a mad man in a straight jacket trying to break free.

Darwin screamed, "I know he's not getting up, but I want to make him feel pain when he wakes up. I don't want him to ever forget this."

Cassady spoke softly to Darwin. "Darwin, buddy. Hey man, they are down. They can't hurt Sean anymore. They can't hurt us. It's over. He won't forget it. I promise."

"Yeah, okay. Yeah, it's over... it's over. They can't hurt us. They can't hurt Sean anymore." Darwin restated his words like an affirmation. He dropped the short metal pipe. It clanked on the concrete and I remembered when his father has given it to him to keep in his car in case any "blacks, rednecks, or crack addicts" ever tried to rob him. Jocks were not on the list.

Ogie stood up, held out his hand and pulled me to my feet. Sean was sitting on the ground crying. One jock started to stand, but sat back down when Darwin looked at him. The other two were now crawling into the yard of a 1950s ranch house. All of us were dirty and bleeding, but the jocks were by far the most beaten.

We walked, no limped, back to school and went home. I drove back to my house and felt the thumping in my back as blood filled the newly forming bruise. Boyhood fights rarely amounted to much. A few punches might be thrown. Boys might tumble through the dirt wrestling until one was pinned, but even the worst of fights I had seen, or been involved in, thus far has been mild. This was my first real fight where the consequences could be high. I was proud to defend Sean—and afraid. When the fight started, adrenaline took over, but I maintained enough control to avoid committing a deathly blow. Darwin had not. If Cassady hadn't pulled him back, he might have killed one or more of the jocks. This realization sent a chill up my spine that numbed and then burned hot when it neared the bruise.

Chapter 14

I didn't know if I was shaking from the cold or because we were sneaking into Mother Elly's empty rental house. I kept telling myself how stupid I was for leaving my jacket in the car, especially on a February night. It didn't feel that cold when I ran from my house to Darwin's car, but since we'd left the car downtown and walked to Mother Elly's, the cold had plenty of time to penetrate my meager clothing. Darwin, Ogie and I thought we could take the girls to Elly's abandoned house, drink a little and then see what might happen next. Our ideas of what might "happen next" were clearly defined in our heads, but we insinuated to the girls that it was just a safe place to drink. The girls probably had their ideas as well.

The shotgun house Elly had rented for years to various tenants was now empty. The last renter, a twenty year old named A.J., had left the house without paying several months of rent. After A.J. was removed by the sheriff's department Elly paid Darwin and me a hundred bucks to clean up the mess. We thought it was easy money, but after spending an entire weekend tossing jars of fluids that looked like they contained human waste, we decided Mother Elly got a deal. The pentagram A.J. had burned into the wooden floor of the shotgun shack was too deep to sand out, so we left it and suggested Elly put down carpet to cover the symbol, a symbol often used by heavy metal rock bands pretending to be Satanists.

Ogie smiled when he turned the door knob and pushed open the solid oak door. "It's not locked."

"That's great," I said. "Remember not to make a mess or burn the place down if you can."

Darwin lit a candle on a mantel in the middle room of the three room house. Shotgun houses were designed for hot climates, with a door in the front of the house and a window at the back. With the streamlined, or straight 'shotgun' shape of the house, air could flow through what were three simple, large high-ceiling rooms. Elly lived in another shotgun house twenty feet from her rental house. Both sat on a hill so that the houses looked down onto the street.

"There we go. Now we have enough light to see our mouths so we can drink," Darwin said and then pulled a plastic bag of weed from his coat pocket. "And to see whatever we need to see. Look what I got. My dad took it from a college student the other day. He tossed it in the trash when he got home and I retrieved it when I took out the trash later. First time that chore has ever paid off."

"Do y'all smoke pot?" Kendi asked looking at Ogie.

"Well, I uh…I don't," Ogie answered like a child in trouble.

"I didn't think so," Kendi responded. "What's that on the floor?" She noticed the fifteen foot diameter pentagram.

"That's a Satanic symbol. Don't know what it means," I said.

"I ain't staying in the same room with that thing, then. Ogie, you get me out of here—now!" Kendi put her arms around Ogie and pulled herself close to him. He smiled in response and put his large arm against her head and pulled it into his chest.

"It's not going to hurt you, baby. Just think of it as bad decorating," Ogie said trying to comfort her.

Darwin shrugged his shoulders and rolled a joint. He lit it and didn't offer it to anyone else. Elena looked at him and I couldn't tell if she was mad, disappointed or ambivalent. She took a beer from her coat pocket and opened it, thus signaling to the rest of us it was time to drink.

"Come sit down with me," Yonah asked, grabbing my hand and pulling me toward the center of the pentagram. "Everyone, come sit with us."

The first beer made me colder, but by the time I finished the second one, the cold embraced me. I let the alcohol relax my body and didn't resist the urge to lie down. Yonah lay down next to me, warming the right side of my body. Kendi was next to Yonah and Ogie next to Kendi. Darwin sat on the floor with his legs crossed and Elena's head resting on his lap. The candle was burning out and in its slow death it created dancing shapes on the ceiling that hypnotized those of us lying on the floor.

"Have you told your parents about Ogie yet?" Elena asked Kendi. It was a question we all wanted to know the answer to, but had been afraid to ask.

Kendi breathed heavy then spoke. "No, not yet. They know I'm sorta going out with someone. They don't know it's serious."

I pulled up at my shoulders and looked at Kendi and said, "Serious? You mean it's serious?" I smiled to let her know I was on her side.

Kendi smiled too, but didn't answer.

"I hope you two get married," Yonah said. "I hope you two get married so we can all hang out together. So we can hang out forever. I don't want to ever meet another person or make another friend. I want to have picnics with the girls while you all go to work. I want to eat at each other's houses on the weekends and watch each other's kids grow up. I don't want anything to change because I don't think it can get any better than this."

"We're on the floor of an abandoned shotgun shack drinking cheap beer. I hope it gets better than this," Darwin said.

"Shut up, Darwin. You know what I mean. Not this house... us."

Elena sat up and asked, "So you two: Ogie. Kendi. When are you going to tell your parents? Are you going to tell them? Someone's going to find out eventually."

"I don't know. I don't know when," Ogie said.

"We'll tell them when we're ready. I don't see a reason to rush it," Kendi said, backing up Ogie. "Are y'all gonna tell? Why do you care anyway?"

"I don't care," I said, trying to keep Kendi from feeling pressured. "It's your business, but if—"

Kendi cut me off. "But if I was white it wouldn't matter. Is that what you were going to say?"

I couldn't respond. I didn't know what to say and wished the topic hadn't been brought up.

"None of you know what it's like to be black." Kendi caught herself and held back her anger. "Y'all are my friends. I know that, but you can't ever understand what my life is like. I can't go anywhere where people don't stare at me. I can't go into a store without the employees watching everything I do."

I was embarrassed. I knew I had to say something. "I didn't know all that Kendi." I thought for a moment about what she said before continuing. "Or maybe I have known. I just haven't thought about it much. I'm sorry. I know now. I know because you're my friend and that's more important than anything else."

Kendi reached over Yonah and hugged me and whispered in my ear, "I know Gus. I know you didn't mean anything bad. We're friends and we can say anything that needs to be said. Okay?"

"Okay. I'll remember that," I whispered back to her.

Ogie sat up straight, his face tightened. "I'm going to tell my parents. I'm going to tell everyone. There's no need to hide this any longer." He looked at Kendi and said, "I love you Kendi. That's all that matters. My father taught me to be a man and that's what I'm going to be. Even if it's not what he expected."

A peace filled me when Kendi smiled in recognition of Ogie's declaration. The tension in the room subsided and we all rested again. The alcohol flowed into my muscles and relaxed me even more. I started to fall asleep.

My mind reached the place between sleep and awake. I was still aware, but gone enough for it to begin the process of dreaming. I first saw the outside of the shotgun shack as I remembered it as a child. High grass surrounded the stone stairs and the smell of fallen and rotting apples filled the air. Then I saw a scene inside the shotgun house not from my memory. Six people in black robes surrounded the pentagram on the floor. The room glowed red, not quite like the light from a candle, but not the light a bulb would emit either. The group in black robes was chanting something I didn't recognize. They passed around a mason jar filled with a red liquid and each drank from the jar. Was it blood? My vision panned to one of the figures and moved toward his face. It was the old resident, A.J. He looked directly into my eyes. I felt I knew the other five, but I didn't recognize them under their black hoods. AJ opened his mouth and a sound like a dog barking blasted from his throat. I awoke quickly and stood up.

"Wow, that was weird," I said and noticed the others in the room looked startled as well. I assumed when I jumped up, it shocked them. "I'm sorry. I didn't mean to scare y'all. I just had a weird dream. I guess it was a dream. Maybe I was imagining."

Yonah stood up and grabbed my arm with her hands. "I saw something weird too."

"Yeah, what did you see?" Kendi asked.

"It was in this room. There was a group of people. Maybe six I think," Yonah said.

Darwin held up his hand for her to stop talking and said, "Was the room dark except for a red glow, a light?"

"That's what I saw," I said.

Yonah finished her description of the vision. "They had on black robes." We shook our head in agreement. "They were standing around this pentagram."

"Yeah, the same one we we're laying on," Ogie stated and his body shook like a chill ran up his spine.

"Did you see it too, Ogie?" Darwin asked.

"Yes. I was pulled toward the leader. I don't know why I know he was the leader, but anyway. I was face to face with him and I couldn't talk or move. I don't think I was in my body. It was like watching a movie, but like being in the movie. I can't explain."

"No need to. I think we all saw it," Yonah said.

Kendi walked through the door into the kitchen and toward the door to the outside. "I'm gone. Y'all can stay as long as you like, but I ain't staying in this haunted house one more second. You coming, Ogie?"

Ogie nodded and we all followed Kendi quickly into the cold February night. The house had been cold, but it had stopped the wind and had been a few degrees warmer making it habitable, until the vision anyway. We stopped at the bottom of the stone steps and I looked up at the window to the room where we had seen the vision.

The candle had burned out, but the room had a faint red glow—a glow we hadn't noticed when we were in the room a few seconds before. A shadow the shape of a human moved in the window. We all jumped and Elena screamed. She hadn't verified that she had seen the vision except through head nods, but her silence was broken when we saw the shadow.

"Just a shadow, just a shadow, but let's go anyway," I said while shifting my weight left to right. I spoke quickly. "It's getting late. We need to get the girls home. Does anyone have a problem with that?"

We were between Mother Elly's shotgun house and the haunted house when a blast echoed between the outside walls like a canon shot in a canyon. Ogie grabbed Kendi, pushed her to the ground and jumped on top of her body. The girls and I froze and Darwin ran for the hill. Darwin was stopped when a power line along the street hit the ground next to the hill and started jumping in all directions like a recently cut lizard tail.

"Who goes there?" A voice yelled to us. It was Mother Elly. "Who goes there? You had better stop running or the next shot is going ta fill your ass with buckshot."

I yelled to keep her from shooting Darwin. "Mother Elly. It's Gus. It's me and my friends. I think you scared Darwin." My heart was racing, but I was trying to talk calmly to ease the situation.

"Well, why didn't you say so, and why are you running around here at night in this cold?" She asked.

I walked to Mother Elly after she lowered her shotgun. "You scared Darwin to death. You scared all of us."

"Well, you shouldn't be sneaking around at night." She started walking back toward her house. "I guess you better come on in. You'll catch a cold out here and die of pneumonia. I'll make some hot chocolate."

Elly flipped the light switch on her kitchen wall several times. When she shot the power line it killed the power to her house. We hadn't noticed the light from her windows going out because we were so frightened. Mother Elly walked to a stand-alone cabinet next to her kitchen door and grabbed three candles and book of matches. Her kitchen was simple with a large white sink with a single faucet, a stove, and an icebox she bought the year my father was born. The sink was attached to the wall and below it was open, exposing the pipes. The ceiling was at least twelve feet high and one window at the end of the room allowed light from the moon to pour in like a flashlight from space. Another window faced the haunted house we'd just fled.

Elly lit the candles and placed them around the kitchen to provide light. She lit the gas stove with a match and within a few minutes water was boiling. Mother Elly poured hot water into mugs and gave each of a paper packet of hot chocolate mix.

"Let's go into the living room. It's warm in there," Elly said walking toward the dark room. I noticed she glanced out the window toward the haunted house. Had she seen something too?

The girls sat together on an old couch covered in hair from a cat that always hid when company arrived. I sat on the down mattress of Elly's dark iron bed. Darwin and Ogie sat on the floor and leaned against the couch where the girls were sitting. On the wall across from the couch was a bookshelf filled with clay jars and a few books.

I had looked in the jars a few times before and they contained dried plants, dried animal parts, and a few liquids. As I looked at the jars I thought about the mason jars of various liquids we had cleaned out of the house next door. They both collected weird things. Was Mother Elly a Satanist like A.J.? I wondered and I was just drunk enough and shocked enough from the vision and the shotgun blast to ask her. Or to at least ask her in a subtle way.

"Mother Elly. Do you believe in God?"

She raised a brow almost as if she expected the question. She walked over to the shelf with the jars and selected an old Bible. "This was my daddy's Bible. His father was a Presbyterian minister. I was taught about God and Jesus when I was younger than you are now. I love and believe in the stories in this sweet book. I keep it near me for comfort. I hope you'll bury me with it."

"So I guess that means you do believe in God," I said and thought for a few seconds about what my mother had said about Elly. "Momma told me you are a Hoodoo priestess."

"What I am is none of her business. She doesn't love me Gus, and if you don't love someone, you can never really understand them. I practice all sorts of things. I'm very spiritual. Don't forget that. But if you want to know, I do practice a little Hoodoo here and there."

"But you don't go to church."

"So what, Gus," she shouted, causing Elena to spill some of her hot chocolate on Darwin's back. "Just cause I don't believe in church doesn't mean I'm not spiritual."

"I don't get it," I said.

"Gus, you can be spiritual and not go to church. I believe in God, I believe in nature, I believe that there's a lot we don't know." She peered straight into my eyes. "There is a lot we don't understand and some of those things can be dangerous. I sure as hell don't think anyone, in any church, really has all the answers. I do know that I've seen things that no preacher has."

"Are you saying church is bad?"

"Heavens, no. Church is a good thing for a lot of people. Many folks need it and why do I have the right to tell them they're wrong. It's not like I have all the answers. But neither do they. Course it ain't my place to tell 'em that. Religion provides a path to God for those that need a little help finding him on their own. Some have a natural connection to God. It's as natural as reading is to you boys, but just 'cause you can read doesn't mean you'll find the best books to read. That's why you need good teachers in your school. They show you what to read. Church is like that. It helps folks find the right books, helps guide 'em. There ain't no need to put any religion down, you see." Elly kissed the Bible and placed it back on the shelf. "Religion has its place, even if it does hurt people sometimes. Course that's only 'cause religion is man-made. Don't get religion and God mixed up, hear me? God is naturally in all of us. Some deny it, others seek him. Some seek him with the help of church. He's there no matter what we do...or don't do."

"I thought you just said you practiced Hoodoo."

"I do, and why do you think Hoodoo ain't Christian?" Mother Elly walked briskly toward me and sat on the bed next to me. "I don't even want to know what they ain't teachin' you in them schools. There are some things that you can't fight – like evil."

There was a hushed silence over all of us. We'd all just shared a vision that was as evil as anything any of us had ever encountered and the hot chocolate didn't do much to calm our nerves.

"You will be touched by evil in this life." Elly's voice was soft as she looked at Yonah then Kendi then Elena. "But you will have to trust that you will know what to do when the time comes." She looked each of us boys in turn, lingering on Darwin. We all quietly sipped our hot chocolate until enough time had passed that we could politely leave – and none of us could wait to get out of there.

"What do y'all think about what Mother Elly said back there?" Ogie asked as we walked back to the car down the dark street.

"I guess there's some truth to what she said about going to church. All I know is that I'm damn sure never going back to that shotgun house," I responded.

Chapter 15

No matter how cold it gets in Georgia from December through February, you can always count on the return of spring in March. This March was no different, with daytime temperatures reaching almost eighty degrees and nights not falling below sixty. Everyone's moods matched the March weather that weekend and it was a great night for a party. Even though Yonah was walking distance from my house, I still drove my car to the next street to pick her up so that her mother would feel better about letting her go to a non-supervised party. The rest of us didn't dare tell our parents there would be no adults at the party, but Yonah had a unique relationship with her mother—an open and honest relationship—that was odd to me when we were children, and as a teenager I still couldn't quite comprehend it.

Dr. Cook, Yonah's mother, had purchased their house just off of Temple Avenue in the early 1970s. She bought it for less than ten-thousand dollars from the family of an old woman that had recently passed away. It was a solid home, but needed updating. Dr. Cook created a timeless home decorated with local antiques and classic furniture. The house felt like a comfortable museum. Even though I'd been to Yonah's home and played in her yard a hundred times as a kid, I had only been in the house a few times, usually when my parents visited. "Kids and antiques don't mix," Dr. Cook would tell us when we wanted to play inside.

When I pulled into the pebble driveway, my nerves bubbled in my stomach causing it to churn and rumble like a boiling pot of vegetable soup. I was awkward around girls, and even though Yonah and I were old friends, picking her up for a date changed the circumstances of our relationship. She was no longer my kid friend next door, but the girl next door. When I met her, she was taller than me with a straight body that didn't look much different from mine, and even if it had been different I wouldn't have noticed, but now she was as much of a woman as she would ever be and the man that was growing in me noticed every curve. As she matured, I grew to appreciate the smoothness of her skin and when we hugged at school, the smell of her hair lingered in my mind long after she left. I heard her voice and saw into her eyes. Everything external and internal that made her a woman stimulated everything that was making me a man. I was sure that she still saw me as the goofy little boy that lived through the woods and I felt like a hobbled calf trying to keep up with its mother.

As I got out of my car, I breathed in and out deeply to relax my beating heart. I saw Yonah wave at me from the second floor of the traditional Southern house. With white planks and black shutters, the house could be conceived as boring, but the wraparound porch and lines of azaleas and twin oaks that guarded the yard made it the envy of everyone on the street. The house was not pretentious as some in town, but still respectable and fitting for a doctor.

The screen door was shut, but the main door was open when I approached, so I peeked into the shadows of the hallway and knocked on the doorframe.

"Gus, come in, come in. You know you don't have to knock," Dr. Cook yelled to me from the living room.

I walked in and waited for my eyes to adjust to the dark hallway. Then, I squeezed them tight, hoping it would speed up the process. Since Dr. Cook had become ill with Lou Gehrig's disease, she kept the lights low. I don't know if the light hurt her eyes or if it simply suited her mood. Dr. Cook wheezed and then coughed. I hid my fear of her sickness when I walked into the room.

"Gus, I'm so glad to see you," she said, reaching out to me. She was lying on the couch with a blanket up to her waist. She wasn't reading or watching TV or doing anything to pass the time. She was just there and this struck me as odd because she was never one to waste a moment of free time. I reminded myself that she probably was too tired to do anything—even to read.

"Dr. Cook, it's good to see you too," I said, trying to smile.

"Sit down, Gus. I want to talk to you before you go. Yonah's upstairs getting ready and even though you don't know it yet, women are never ready on time, so we have a while to talk." The last few words were slurred.

"Okay, I guess I'll get comfortable then," I said sitting in a dark red-leather, winged back chair. "So, how are you doing?"

"I'm fine...well, I'm dying, but other than that I'm doing swell." She laughed then coughed.

"I'm sorry. I didn't –"

"I know what you meant, Gus. I'm sorry. I shouldn't have made you uncomfortable. I have a sick sense of humor, and to be honest, I get in bad moods about this disease sometimes."

"Anyone would."

"I know," she said. "But I'm not anyone. I'm me."

"Yeah, I know," I said feeling embarrassed and wishing Yonah would come down to rescue me.

"I'm sorry, Gus. I just did it again. I'm being a real bitch to you and you were only being kind. I'm a doctor. I should be better with death than this."

"Don't be sorry, Dr. Cook. I don't know what I would do if it were me."

Dr. Cook tried to push herself up straight, but her arms failed her. I started to get up to help her but she held her hand up. She stopped trying to adjust her body and said, "I know I'm supposed to say something about how I'm doing great with death, how I've accepted it and come to terms with it. Well, that's bullshit. I don't want to die. I'm not finished."

I looked directly into her eyes as she spoke. I knew she was opening up to me and I didn't want her to feel I didn't care, but inside I wanted the conversation to end. With one ear I listened to the doctor and with the other, I longed to hear Yonah's footsteps on the stairs. I had to say something, so I said what was in my heart at that moment.

"I'll take care of Yonah after you're gone. I'll make sure she has a good life."

Dr. Cook smiled and said, "I know you will Gus, but don't do that for me, or even for her. Something that big has to be done because you want to—not out of obligation—or you'll resent her for it later. Maybe much later, but later. Just be her friend when she needs it, Gus. That's all I ask of you."

"Yes ma'am."

"Not that I wouldn't be happy to see her with you. You're a fine young man," she said before her face grew tight and angry again. "I want to see my girl go to college, to get married. I want to be a grandmother and spoil her children. But I'm getting robbed. It's all bullshit. There's no reason. God isn't involved in this. It's just happening and there's no reason—God, Satan, or otherwise."

I heard Yonah's door open upstairs. Now that she was on her way, I wanted her to remain upstairs longer.

"You would think that I would have wanted to climb mountains, see Europe, or do something spectacular now that I'm dying, but I don't. I just want to be with the people I love. That's it. I have Yonah. She is the best thing I've ever done. She's the only thing that matters. So if you're looking for some reason for life in my end of life rant here it is: to love. That's it, Gus. My college degrees, my career—none of it matters. None of it. The only thing that's worth it is my little girl. She's my heart and my life. She's what's made this painful trip on earth worth it. She's my joy. Everything else…everything else you can toss in a bag and ship it to China."

The doctor looked through the door to the staircase where Yonah was bouncing down like a spring bunny. She was wearing a tight pair of acid washed jeans, a yellow tank top and a black leather jacket. I stood up and met her at the door, where she grabbed my hand and lead me over to the couch.

Her mother grabbed each of our free hands and looked up at us. I expected more end of life words, but instead she said, "Don't do anything you'll regret tonight, but if you do, maybe it'll mean I get to meet my grandchild before I die."

"Mother, that's not funny. I can't believe you said that," Yonah responded as I felt my ears growing hot.

"Well, it was nice to see you again Dr. Cook. We have to get going now so we don't miss the party," I said.

"Oh Gus, you're so funny. How can you be late to a party that goes all night long? You two get out of here. And Yonah..."

"Yes, mother?"

"Don't drink and drive and don't get in the car with anyone that is drinking, even a little."

Outside, I opened the door for Yonah and almost jumped over the hood of my 1966 Mustang on my way back to the driver's side. I was elated to be free and my loins were heating up after seeing Yonah in her tight clothes. She knew she had me and she was working every move and word to keep me going like a rocket about to leave the planet.

"Do you think I'm pretty?" she asked.

"Yes, I think you're very pretty. I think you're beautiful."

"Really? I'm glad you said that. I've never had a boy call me beautiful before."

"You've always been beautiful, but right now you're also very sexy."

"Yeah?"

"Yeah, and I like it."

She leaned over and kissed me on the neck and then whispered, "I'm sexy just for you."

Chapter 16

"Where did you get all that liquor?" Darwin asked as he and Elena approached us.

Ogie smiled and proudly said, "I used the Kyle Jeowitz ID I got from my cousin in college."

"Who's Kyle Jeowitz?" Darwin asked.

"I don't know, but it says here that he lives in Buffalo Grove, Illinois and that he was born in 1962. Do I look 28 to any of you?"

"No, you don't even look 21," I said.

"Yeah, that's what I think too, but the Chinese dude at the Happy Stop doesn't care as long as I've got something to get him off the hook. I heard if you're a good looking girl you can show him your movie rental card and he'll take it. My ass isn't tight enough, so I had to use this ID."

"Oh, don't put yourself down. I love your ass," Kendi said as she reached over and pinched Ogie's butt, causing him to drop his beer.

"I'm with Kendi. I think your ass is great," Darwin said before taking one of Ogie's contraband beers from an open cooler. "Course, I'll say anything nice to the one that brings the beer."

Cassady's boss, from the dry cleaners where he worked after school, had asked him to babysit his house while he was on vacation. It wasn't the best idea and we wondered why he didn't think Cassady would have a party at the house.

The house was only a few years old and had been built with money made from gas stations and dry cleaners. It was white stucco with two columns in front of a large cherry wood door. A large window above the door displayed a chandelier that cost more than what my parents had paid for our house. It was comfortable inside and decorated with white tiles, brass and green leather furniture. It was modern, but not so much that it didn't fit in with the other homes of Longwood Road. Behind the house was a pool with a grotto and a waterfall covering the grotto's entrance. Around the pool was a fence and plants designed to hide the pool. Not that this was needed, however, as the nearest neighbor was an acre away.

Cassady's boss, Mr. Morrison, had built his wealth from nothing. First a dry cleaning business and then a series of gas stations strategically located around Caswell County. Mr. Morrison was new money and didn't fit in with the old money of River Falls, but that was fine as he didn't care. He was one of the few true millionaires I knew and my impression of him was much different from people with a fraction of his wealth. Mr. Morrison was relaxed, friendly and without any pretension. While the old money of River Falls was the definition of snotty, the man with true wealth showed none of it in his person. Because of this, I admired and respected Mr. Morrison, but my desire to have a party without an adult overcame any guilt I had about drinking in his house while he was on vacation.

We each had our girlfriends and had staked out a bedroom earlier that day, before picking up the girls. Prior to picking up Yonah, I had no illusion of anything happening when I selected a windowless basement room, but after Yonah's whispers I was now optimistic. Kendi and Ogie laid claims to Morrison's teenage boy's bedroom and I was sure that the clumsy fourteen year old had never done anything in his room that resembled what would soon be happening. I'd assumed Cassady would sleep alone in the master bedroom until I heard a familiar voice.

"Heaay, anybody in there?" Chastity stretched out every vowel as she yelled. "Somebody come get me. I can't find my way through this big ole' mansion."

"Back here. Follow my voice," Cassady yelled back.

"I'd prefer you follow the light," I said, but only loud enough for the group at the table to hear. Cassady looked my way and I thought he was mad until he smiled.

"Why don't you like her?" Yonah asked me.

"No particular reason. Why do you think I don't like her?" I asked. Yonah shrugged her shoulders and I saw Kendi look toward the pool so Yonah couldn't see her face.

Chastity was wearing a tight leather miniskirt and a Metallica t-shirt. The temperature was warm, but I still thought it was too cold to wear such a short skirt. She was smacking gum when she came outside. Before she had time to make eye contact with the group, Cassady walked to her, pushed her body against the wall and started kissing her. Cassady had been swimming in the heated pool and his towel fell from his shoulders when she pulled him to her.

"Well, I guess that's it for the hellos," Kendi said.

"I think I might go shake her hand," Elena responded. "Maybe give her a hug."

Darwin said, "Yes, yes. I think greetings are in order." Darwin raised his voice. "Hello Chastity. Hello. We would like to welcome you to our orgy, I mean party. We didn't know you were coming."

Cassady lifted his hand and waved us off as he continued to kiss and grind Chastity against the wall.

Darwin stood up and walked close to the grinding couple. "What's the problem, Cassady? Are you telling us to leave you two alone? I'm not sure. I can't hear what you're saying over all the slurping. I do think that you might be hurting that poor girl, and if not her, I'll bet you're doing some real damage to Mr. Morrison's stucco. You should check to see if she still has her gum because I think it's stuck to your chest. Wait, never mind, that's just your nipple."

Cassady gently pushed away from his date. "Sorry, I forgot my manners. She's staying the night with us. Me, I mean she's staying the night with me." Cassady was embarrassed to admit she was going to stay overnight with him, and I found this odd as he hadn't been embarrassed to make out in front of us.

"Awesome," I responded. Chastity noticed my sarcasm and shot me a bird.

"And fuck you too, girly," I shot back in response to her gesture.

Her face tightened and she leaned hard on one foot. "What's your problem with me? You were sure friendly when you thought you could get in my pants. In fact, I want to know what's everyone's problem? I haven't done a thing to one of you other than try to have fun."

Elena stood up and grabbed Chastity's hand. "I'm sorry. Gus didn't mean anything by it. He's just sexually frustrated." I noticed Elena's cheeks turn red after her sarcastic remark.

"I'm not sorry," I said in quick response.

"You're not? Why not?" Chastity asked. I was about to respond with another smart ass remark when I noticed her eyes watering. Tears were not falling, but her eyes glistened with sadness. There's not much that bothers me, but a girl crying is right up there with dying puppies in the list of things most likely to break me down.

"Ahh, great," I said under my breath and then looked at Cassady and apologized with my eyes, and just in time, too, because when I looked at him I could see the veins in his neck expanding. "Look Chastity, I'm sorry. I am. I don't know why I'm mean to you."

Chastity relaxed her shoulders and put her arm around Cassady, who had moved close to her again. "It's okay, Gus. I don't like embarrassing y'all. I just want to have fun. You are the only people I can relax around. I hate being at home. My daddy drinks too much and I have to spend every night of my life listening to him rant on and on until he passes out. He's an old drunk. I love him and he can be real sweet when he ain't drinking, but I don't get to see much of that anymore." I looked to Elena, hoping she would say something as I had no idea how to respond.

"Okay...well I think it's time to order a pizza," Elena said. "Pepperoni okay with everyone?"

"It's time for shots. Who wants a Seminole Twist?" Cassady asked holding up his hands like a cha-cha dancer. "It's part Vodka and part schnapps. The schnapps is fruity and covers up the rubbing alcohol taste of the vodka."

"I'm in," Ogie said.

"Yep, me too," I said, hoping the alcohol would save the party I almost destroyed.

The shots were followed by beer and then more shots. I never understood the need for drinking games, but we played a few anyway. Maybe it made it easier for the girls to drink, allowing them to release the weight of their conservative Southern upbringings that still held hints of the Victorian era of extreme modesty and composure. Young males were always allowed flexibility and forgiveness and were expected to break the rules. It was even laughed at when we were caught by the police or busted making out with a girl behind the house, but for the girls, the double standard was real and pervasive. If they were busted with a guy, it could mean a destroyed reputation. A laugh and a pat on the back was the reward for the males, while the girls were rewarded with a reputation that could follow them for years. The times were changing and we didn't care as much about these things as our parents did, but the old ways were still present and busting through the old ways took the magic of illegally obtained alcohol that allowed the girls to forget about the double standard for at least one night. In the morning, they would suffer from both a hangover and guilt, but that was later and this was the night.

Cassady's Florida State inspired shot, combined with the beers, sent my mind and body into a place of relaxation, or Zen really. No worries, no inhibitions, no fears, no future, no past. Being drunk was a new sensation and one I would relish throughout out my teenage and young adult years. The magic elixir connected me with God while a tape from the band U2 was playing on the pool sound system. Every song felt like it lasted twenty minutes. The girls were giggling to each other about something and I smiled at them, causing the laughter to grow louder like a group of seagulls swarming bread on the beach. Ogie slid his fingers behind Kendi and up her shirt and stroked her back gently. He looked over at me and offered an opium smile. Darwin was staring at his bare feet. His brow and face were tightened with a seriousness that gave the appearance of someone who had just discovered the secrets of the universe. We were on a different plane. We were one in a manner only a Buddhist could appreciate.

While I was floating in my buzz, the girls were planning something that would bring their dates back to reality and send us to Heaven all at once. Chastity, being the least modest, took off her Metallica t-shirt and pulled down her miniskirt. Immediately, I forgot why I didn't like her and gazed upon her body and her red bikini. It was a wondrous sight that became better when the other girls undressed as well, offering four beautiful bodies covered only in well-fitting bikinis. Yonah's yellow bikini matched her hair and she held her face down and looked up sporadically revealing the glow in her cheeks. Elena's naturally tanned body and black hair fell to just above her breast. Kendi had larger hips than the other girls and her dark skin blended with her brown bikini suggesting nudeness. The site of the four was a buffet of pleasure for our teenage eyes.

The girls jumped into the heated pool, breaking the fog that hovered over the water in the cool night air. I remained at the table with the guys and enjoyed the view of the angelic creatures swimming in the night. Yonah swam under water to the grotto, and before swimming through the waterfall, she looked through the mist and invited me without words to join her in the warm cave.

"Son, I think you oughta get your ass in that water," Cassady said to me before drinking a shot of straight vodka.

"Yep," I responded. There was little to say.

My eyes adjusted to the dim light inside the grotto and I saw water dripping from Yonah's face. It was not pool water but tears. She was so happy a moment before and was now crying.

"What's wrong? Are you not having fun?" I asked.

"No, nothing's wrong. I'm having a blast."

"Something's wrong. You're crying."

"I'm just a little drunk. Girls sometimes cry when they're drunk," she said.

"I didn't know that. I don't much about girls, I guess."

"No, I guess you don't, Gus."

I pushed through the warm water next to Yonah. She put her arms around my waist and her head on my shoulder. Her wet hair was cold when it touched my neck, causing me to shiver. I thought her skin was softer than anything I'd ever felt before as I moved my hands up her back and I realized this was the first time I had ever touched the naked back of a woman.

She spoke.

"My mother is going to die."

"I know. I'm sorry."

"There's no reason for you to be sorry. No one is to blame. It's just the world. It's reaching her lungs now. She'll be dead soon. She could use machines to stay alive, but she doesn't want that. She's going to let it take her. My mother told me that she wants the pain for me to be over sooner, but I told her I didn't care. I told her I want her to live. To see me graduate college, to get married, to have kids. Doesn't matter. She wants it over. It doesn't matter what I say, because she has her mind made up."

"I wish I could do something to make it better," I said.

"You can."

"What? I'll do anything. What do you want me to do?"

She kissed me and I tasted the pool's chlorine on her lips and vodka on her breath. She said, "Make love to me. You can make love to me. That will make things better, at least some things."

There were bedrooms in the house, but Yonah wanted her first time to be among the trees, so I went to Ogie's car and took out an old Army duffle bag that contained several blankets and rushed back to Yonah, who was at the edge of the woods waiting for me. She had pulled her clothes over her wet body. Her hair was dripping and the wetness caused her tank top to cling to her breasts like plastic wrap. As sexy as she had been in the pool, she was even more so now. At that moment, I learned that it was women, and not men, who controlled the game of sex. All the bravado of males meant nothing in the end because it was the females that decided who received, like a banker handing out loans. It would happen when and where the female intended and all the animal displays and cockiness were wasted unless the girl was interested.

The others had gone inside, maybe to their respective bedrooms, but I didn't know or care. She held my hand and walked me into the woods just far enough to become invisible from the lights of the house. The radio was blasting Def Leppard as I spread out the thickest blanket on the ground. Yonah laid back on the blanket, lifting herself up on her elbows, and I spread two more blankets over her like I was preparing the ground for a picnic. It was warm when I crawled under the blankets and felt her hot and wet body. We kissed as several songs played in the distance.

"What do you want in a girlfriend?" Yonah asked me.

"I think it would be great if she's not related to me."

She laughed.

"I don't know why, but when you make me laugh it turns me on."

"Ogie laughs at my jokes too. I hope he's not getting turned on."

She laughed again and then kissed me. Her soft lips pressed hard against mine; her tongue filled my mouth. I put my hand on her shoulder, and followed her neckline and worked my fingers to the back of her head beneath her blonde hair.

This wasn't our first kiss, but I tingled like a boy who had never seen a girl before.

It became too hot under the sheets, so I lifted up on my knees and she did the same. Yonah pulled my shirt apart quickly, snapping the buttons revealing my chest. My shirt fell from my arms to the ground. I felt her satin skin with both of my hands as I moved up her side, past her breast and up her skyward pointing arms to remove her wet tank top.

I fumbled with the back of her bikini top, causing her to laugh again. She took control and removed it herself. We both rolled to the ground and onto our backs while pulling our tight jeans off at the same time. She was now wearing underwear—white lace. I had only seen one other girl in her underwear before, when I surprised Cassady and Chastity on New Years, but this was different, and the vision caused the blood to pump hard through my body. My head swam.

It was my first time, her first time and our first time feeling the joining of two bodies into one. I moved in her as nature and God watched and felt her quiver beneath me as I did my best to please her and to get it right.

I knew no secrets and had no experience, so I followed the animal instincts inside of me. She pushed up against my hips and thrashed until I released and fell into her wet body.

After we made love, we pulled one of the blankets over us and looked up through a break in the trees at the stars. I asked her, "Does this mean you're my girlfriend?"

"I don't think so, but it does mean we're really good friends."

"I'm really good friends with Ogie."

"Will you stop bringing him up during our intimate times."

"Sorry, I haven't had too many intimate times before. I don't know what you're supposed to say."

"You can talk about anything."

"Okay. So what does this mean? I mean…for us?"

"It means whatever you want it to mean, but I don't want to get into a relationship right now. Things are too complicated at home. Is that okay?"

"Yeah, I guess it's okay," I said lying. "But why did you ask me what I wanted in a girlfriend then?"

She was quiet for a moment before speaking. "I wanted to pretend, I think. I wanted to feel like your girlfriend in that moment. Why do you care anyway? You just got laid without having to commit. Isn't that what every guy wants?"

I laughed, but wanted her to be sure that it did mean something to me so I said, "That's not true. I'm committed to you. I'm committed in ways that I can't explain. Ways I don't understand. Anyway, I don't think that's what every guy wants. Some do want something real. We talk a big game, but that's about it."

She put her finger on my lips and said, "You don't have to explain. I understand."

I had finally broken through the glass wall and was now among the majority of the world that had practiced the art of love making. I felt like I had just been born again and was among the few who were allowed to experience the ultimate pleasure offered by the Almighty Himself.

Sex had been so elusive until now. In my home, we didn't talk about sex. It wasn't talked about in the classroom either. I knew all the dirty words pertaining to intercourse by the time I was eight and I knew it was bad taste to use them around adults, but I only had a vague idea of their meanings. By the time I was twelve, I had seen enough smuggled porn to know what sex was, understood the science behind baby making and the concept of copulation, but I still lacked anecdotal experience. In my desire to better grasp the allusive art, I spent my teenage years seeking first-hand research and experimentation.

Finding research partners, however, was difficult, as most girls didn't seem as interested in researching—at least not with me. My father once warned me of girls that were easy and would want to take advantage of me and I longed for these sirens of the night, but found none. Finally, after what felt like a lifelong struggle I had tasted the fruit—and I liked it.

Chapter 17

I slept most of the next day and dreamed of making love to Yonah.

I dreamed of sleeping with her, touching her, smelling her. The feeling of being next to a woman all night was new. It was wonderful and I wanted to sleep with her again.

I arrived at school early Monday morning and placed a single red rose in Yonah's locker. I had watched her open it a hundred times before and had memorized the combination. Inside, she had a picture of her mother and her together. Yonah was younger, maybe thirteen. It had only been a few years ago but Dr. Cook looked twenty years younger in the picture than she did now. She was slightly plump with clear skin. The sun reflected off her hair. Yonah was smiling, but her smile looked peaceful—a peace I didn't see now. Her eyes looked so much older now. Older like an adult, not a teenager.

I sat next to Darwin and waited for Yonah to come to class. "How you doing buddy?" Darwin smiled like a movie villain.

"I'm fine, what do you mean?"

"You know what I mean. Do you feel different? Do you feel like a man now?"

"Man, stop it. I don't feel any different at all." I stopped myself and thought for a moment before finishing. "Well, you know what. I guess I do feel different. I can't explain it. I feel like I just crossed a boundary, like I passed some test for adulthood."

"Cool, man. Welcome to the club," Darwin said.

"What club?" Yonah asked. I hadn't seen her come in.

"Nothing, umm, no club. We were just talking," I said.

"I hope you weren't talking too much," Yonah responded and I looked up to see her holding her rose.

Darwin looked at her flower and then at me. "That sure is nice. Who gave you that?"

She looked at me and smiled. "I don't know. I have a secret admirer."

Yonah sat down beside me and touched my hand. Her touch was soft and almost imagined, like satin falling over your body during sleep. Her perfume overcame me and blood pulsed through my body like a fire hose being pumped with water. Her presence was an aphrodisiac and I felt like a boy who had just found his father's Playboy magazine. I sat up straight and tried to drink in the feeling she created. I wondered if every girl had this power or if it was her special gift, her gift to me.

"We need to talk after school," she told me at the end of class. Did my flower bring her over to the idea of a relationship? I could see no other option for us. We had made love. Some teenagers were screwing, but we had shared a real moment. We had bonded, become one. This was our time. I was sure of it.

I met her at her car and sat in the passenger seat. Usually she was giddy, but she sat for the first minute – what felt like an hour – looking out the front windshield at the baseball team practicing.

"Gus," she began. "I like you. I even love you. I picked you to give my virginity to, but—"

"Uh oh, here it comes." I snapped.

"I'm not trying to make you mad, Gus. I'm not."

"I know, but—"

"Look, just, it's just that…" She stopped herself and gathered her thoughts. "Anyway, Gus, like I said. I'm not trying to make you mad, or hurt you."

"But there is a but," I said and exhaled.

She touched my face. "But this isn't going to work. I love the flower. It was thoughtful of you. You've always been good to me. If I was like any other girl, you'd be the one I would want. You would be. But…but I'm not like anyone else."

"I know. That's why I want you."

"Want me, Gus? Do you love me, Gus?"

"Love you?" I asked. "Of course I love you. I uh, I dream of you."

She smiled and I could tell she was flattered. "Thank you, sweet boy. Thank you for loving me like only you can. I'm in a different world than you, sweet boy. We live in the same town and have the same friends, but I live with realities. I hide behind optimism. I hide behind my smiles, but there is pain that is too much for you."

"Too much? I don't know if I really know what love is, Yonah, but I do know what friendship is and I know I want to share your pain with you. I want to help you."

"I can't be helped. I'm just who I am, living in the world I live in. It just is."

"Life sucks," I said.

"No it doesn't Gus. Just parts of it. Friday night didn't suck did it?"

"No, it didn't suck," I said while fighting a smile.

"Things will be better for me someday. Eventually my mother will die. I'll be sad and then I'll deal with it. I'll move on and do great things."

"Like what? What great things?" I asked.

"I don't know yet. Part of the fun is finding out. Maybe someday I'll regret letting you go. I probably will, but I don't know. I just don't know yet."

I looked at her. She was staring out the windshield again at the baseball players.

"If I had tight pants on like the baseball players would things be different?"

She laughed.

A tear rolled down my cheek.

Chapter 18

Yonah tapped my hand to get my attention and nodded her head behind us. The car radio was blasting at full volume and I hadn't noticed Ogie and Kendi making out in my backseat. Yonah's head faced forward while her eyes focused on the rear view mirror. The peep show was too much for her to resist. I leaned over to Yonah and whispered, "Make sure your seat belt is on. I'm going to run off the road and hit the horn."

Yonah mouthed, "Why?"

"Just do it," I mouthed back before slowly pulling the seatbelt over my lap. My old Mustang didn't have a shoulder strap, but it didn't matter as I rarely even wore the seatbelt.

I waited till the next song started on the radio and looked in the mirrors to make sure no other cars were around, then I screamed, slammed on the brakes and slid into the gravel parking lot of a defunct gas station. The car went from 45 mph to 0 in seconds and the change in gravity hurled Ogie and Kendi into the back of our seats. The tires screeched before hitting the gravel that caused the car to fishtail before coming to a complete stop.

Yonah smiled, not sure if she should laugh, but I was laughing so hard I had to remove my lap belt and exit the car. Ogie followed me out, tripping to the ground. His shirt was un-tucked and his pants unbuttoned. His hair was a mess, and for a second, I was reminded of the first time I met him. Kendi was on the back floorboard on all fours. She used the back of Yonah's seat to right herself and then exited the car behind Ogie.

Kendi's eyes tightened and she shook her head while looking at the ground before erupting. "You crazy fucker. What the hell were you thinking?" Her outburst made me laugh so hard I bent forward. "What's so damn funny, you stupid fucking white boy?"

Kendi stopped. Her anger dissipated. I could see that she was worried she had offended me and maybe even her boyfriend. Ogie and I stopped laughing like a light being turned off. Yonah sat still in her seat looking out the car window in the opposite direction. It was an odd and uncomfortable few seconds before Ogie broke the tension.

"Stupid fucking white boy. Yes, I agree. Gus is one stupid fucking white boy." While Ogie usually used his verbal genius to insult teachers and those he felt were below his mental ability, he was now using it for good.

I put my arm around Kendi's shoulder and asked, "Do you really think I'm a stupid fucking white boy?"

She placed her arm behind my back and squeezed. "No, but I do think you're fucking stupid."

"Ahhh, thanks. That's the nicest thing anyone has ever said to him," Ogie responded.

"Thanks a lot, you two. If I wanted this kind of abuse, I would have called my mother. Okay, okay. I'm sorry. It was just too easy. I guess next time, you'll think twice before getting nasty in the back seat of my car."

Yonah leaned over the driver seat and asked, "What's so wrong with getting nasty in your car?"

I felt my ears turn hot, again. Yonah was making a habit of embarrassing me.

"Looks like someone is embarrassed," Kendi said.

"Want me to drive so you can make out in the back seat now?" Ogie asked.

"If you don't mind, but I'm not sure Yonah will like me kissing another girl."

"Oh, you funny man," Yonah said. "Go ahead and kiss anyone you want. I'm not your girlfriend."

"Then I guess that means you're my—" I stopped myself from responding in a way that would end the double date prematurely. I wanted to ask her why we slept together if she wasn't my girlfriend, but I knew that would definitely end any chance of ever being with her again. Girls were complicated and Yonah was even more complicated. I figured if I could deal with her, then the rest of my life with women would be easy.

Ogie noticed the mess I almost got myself into and quickly changed the subject. "Y'all ready to go? I want to get a good seat for the movie." Again, he had used his art of articulation to save the world. Our world anyway.

I wondered why people were staring at us when we arrived until I remembered our double date included a black girl. A few months before, I would have stared too, but now there was something new inside of me and that new creature in me knew and loved Kendi as a friend and that creature wanted to lash out. Instead, I focused on holding my head high and my body straight. I was not going to let anyone hurt the ones I loved with their negative thoughts. Ogie was my best friend and I was going to protect my friend and his girl from the ignorant, even if only with my pride.

Smugness overcame me as I thought highly of myself for being one of the few who had broken an unwritten law. I was Kendi's friend and my best friend was dating her. I told myself how evolved I was, how superior I was to the simple-minded. I wanted whites to envy me for overcoming my superstitions and fears and for rebelling against the status quo and I wanted the praise of blacks for being brave enough to cross invisible boundaries. I felt better than everyone around me and I didn't care.

"Look at that boy. I guess he can't get it from a white girl," a voice said from a few rows behind. The guy was not alone. I had seen him and his two friends in the lobby before we entered the theatre. One was wearing a trucker hat with a picture of a deer and plaid shirt that made him look like the most stereotypical redneck in history. When he snickered at us as we walked by in the lobby, I wondered why anyone with such a stupid looking hat was laughing at anyone else. In the lobby I held my tongue, but now

I was incensed. How dare anyone say, or even suggest, anything negative about me or my friends, I thought. Yonah grabbed my arm and pulled me down when I stood up.

"Don't stop me. They can't say shit like that," I said to her. An older lady a few rows ahead turned around and put her finger to her mouth.

"Ignore them," Kendi said to me and I was about to comply, but it was too late. Ogie was out of his seat and in the center aisle. He grabbed the stereotypical redneck by the neck and lifted him from his seat and into the isle. The commotion caused people behind and next to us to stand up and bunch together like chickens in a chicken house hiding from a fox. Those in rows in front of us hadn't seen or heard the disturbance and continued watching the movie until Ogie dropped the trucker hat instigator on the ground. The redneck was on all fours holding his neck while coughing. For a moment, I thought the fight would be over because the other two rednecks sat in their seats stunned, but I was wrong as it didn't take long for them to realize what was happening.

"Oh hell, man. Look what you done did. You're going down boy. I'm gonna break your face." The second redneck stood up and leapt over the seats in front of him that were now empty.

I moved toward the aisle to help Ogie when a punch caught the side of my face and sent me to the floor next to the gasping redneck. My vision grew dark and I thought I was going to pass out, but managed to shake it off and regain balance. Before he could hit me a second time, Yonah grabbed his mullet and pulled hard enough to drop him to his knees. Now he was between my row and the seats behind us. I knew this was my only chance to return fire, so I punched down on the top of his head with all my strength. Electric charges echoed through my hand and wrist, but the hit also sent him to the butter-coated floor. He didn't get up.

Ogie made sure the man he had pulled out of the seat by the neck couldn't recover by kicking him hard in the ribs. The remaining redneck pulled a knife from his pocket, but there was no way he could open the knife before Ogie grabbed the man's belt buckle with one hand and the top of his shirt with the other. Ogie bent his knees and lifted the redneck over his head with the agility of an Olympic weightlifter performing a clean and jerk maneuver. Then Ogie carried the offender down the aisle until they reached the screen. Ogie bent his knees slightly again before blasting the redneck above his head and into the movie screen. The man's body ripped a human sized gash in the screen before bouncing to the ground. Anyone that had been too entranced with the movie to notice the fight before couldn't miss it now. There was a collective gasp, then a series of screams from the audience.

The violence in the film hadn't effected the moviegoers, but a moment of real violence had sent them scrambling from the room. The panicked group emptied the theatre, where they bottlenecked at the two doors leading to the lobby. I knew we were going to be arrested if we stayed, so I grabbed Yonah and Kendi and ran with them toward the exits near the front of the theatre.

When we reached Ogie, the movie screen redneck was bleeding from his hairline and nose and was cowered against the wall under the ripped screen. The movie continued to play and gunshots from the speakers bounced around the emptying room.

"You asked for it. You asked for it. You did this. You made me do this. You asked for it." Ogie was repeating his words to the man that was no longer a threat to us, or anyone.

"Ogie, baby. Ogie. Let's go. Let's go before someone comes in here." Kendi was stroking Ogie's back.

"Yeah, okay. Let's go." Ogie looked at Kendi and then at me. "You drive. I'm shaking."

The exit doors lead us to the back of the theatre. The parking lot had been full when we arrived, so we had parked near the back. This was a bit of luck that probably saved us from being noticed as we slipped quietly into my Mustang. I told the others to duck down to reduce our chances of being noticed as a group. I pulled onto the road at the parking lot exit farthest from the front doors of the movie theatre and we were still in sight of the building when four police cars raced past us.

"I used to get my brothers to fight for me when I needed it," Kendi said smiling at Ogie. "But now I have you. You're my protector. You protect me from this evil world."

Chapter 19

Yonah was crying when I answered the phone. Phone calls in the middle of the night were rarely good and my heart raced before I picked up the receiver. After a few seconds, I dropped the receiver and ran out my back door, across my yard and into the woods toward her house. I almost slipped in mud behind her house before jumping up the rock stairs and into her backdoor. Her mother was now gone. She had been taken to an assisted living facility on the other side of town a few days before. Because Yonah only had a few months until high school graduation, she was allowed to live on her own. While running, I assumed, hoped, she was sad about her mother being gone. I hoped she was only lonely. I was wrong. It was so much more.

With no relatives to go to, her only other option was a foster home. The lawyer appointed to oversee her and her mother, Taft Gregory, volunteered to check in on Yonah every few days and to ensure she had food and other important needs. Yonah didn't trust Gregory and suspected he was stealing from her mother's estate, but there was no way to prove it because Gregory was friends with the Probate Judge, Rush, who refused to investigate or have the account audited. I told Yonah she should tell her mother, but she refused not wanting to upset her. "At least Taft is letting me stay home and not go into foster care," she told me.

The clock on the microwave displayed 12:42 AM when I ran through the kitchen toward the front foyer. I started up the stairs to Yonah's room when I heard her call to me from the living room, the same room where I had spoken to her mother about death. Yonah was curled up on the couch where her mother had spent so many long days. A quilted blanket was wrapped around her. I was shocked to see dried blood under her nose and her left eye dark blue and swelling. I stopped at the doorway and froze.

There are moments in life when I haven't known what to say or to do—moments that I knew would change my life. My brain calculated a hundred reasons why she was hurt, but the real reason was beyond my ability to generate. My body wanted to run, but my heart kept me there. I broke free of the self-imposed straightjacket and walked to her and knelt next to the couch. I put my hand on her shoulder. She wouldn't look at me.

"Are you okay?" I asked. "What, what happened?"

She didn't answer my question. "I'm so glad you were my first. I'm glad we had that night together. That's the only reason I'm alive now."

"I don't understand," I said, but I did understand. At least, I was starting too. "Did someone hurt you?"

Again, Yonah didn't answer my question. "Any girl would be lucky to have you."

"That's nice of you to say, but from what I know most girls aren't interested in 120 pound guys with bad skin." I tried to make her smile and she tried to smile for me.

"We can't be together anymore." She said this like she was breaking up with me, but I knew this was more than a simple relationship issue.

Yonah looked up at the ceiling and gasped before letting out a moan that carved itself into my memory. Tears rolled down her face that I wanted to wipe away, but I didn't for fear of hurting her eye.

"He raped me, Gus. He made me. I tried to stop him and he made me do it. I tried to fight him off. I really did, but he hit me. I didn't want to get hit again."

"Who? Who did this to you?" I asked, feeling anger rise. I wanted revenge.

"Taft. That lawyer that's supposed to be taking care of me."

"That…" I bit my lip and stood up. I walked to the door again. I wanted to kill him. If he had been in the house, I would have.

"It started when I questioned him about my mother's money. I called him and told him to show me the books. I asked him to show me the books and to show me that I was wrong. He came over. He came over late, but I thought he was going to finally come clean. Or maybe to show me where I was wrong." Yonah's chest was jumping and her voice shaking. "When he came over, I asked him to show me the books, or something. He didn't have anything with him. I kept asking him to prove to me he wasn't stealing and he got mad, really mad. He started pointing his finger in my face so I slapped his hand. Then he hit me in the stomach and I fell on the floor. I told him I was sorry. I told him I wouldn't bother him about it again. I don't know why, but that just made him even madder."

I walked back to her and sat beside her on the couch. I felt like I was outside my body as I listened to her story of what happened next.

"He jumped on top of me and ripped my shirt open. I didn't think he was really going, really going to…"

I stopped her. "You don't have to tell me this. You need to tell the police. I'll call them now." I started to get up but she pulled me back to the couch.

"He grabbed me hard so I hit him in the face and busted his nose, so he hit me in the nose. I told him to stop or I would tell the police and he told me there was nothing I could do. He told me he knew more police than I did and they would ignore a little slut like me." She stopped and calmed herself before saying more. "He said, 'You couldn't stop me from fucking your retarded mother. How do you think you're going to stop me from fucking you?' And he did."

I tried to make sense of it all for her, for me. "That was an attack Yonah. It wasn't sex. It was nothing more than a crime committed by a senseless animal that deserves to be put down. Yonah, we have to tell someone. We have to call the police. We can call Darwin's father. He'll know what to do, and he'll protect you. He doesn't put up with dirty cops. He won't let anyone else hurt you."

"You can't. Not now. No, not ever. We can't tell anyone. I'm telling you because…I don't know why. I have to tell someone. I can't tell my mother and if we tell the police, she'll find out. She's dying, Gus. We can't tell her. She can't know. I don't want her to die knowing that she couldn't protect me. Knowing that this happened."

"But you didn't do anything wrong. We have to stop that terrible man. That animal. He…"

"No," Yonah snapped. "No, Gus. We will never tell anyone. You have to promise. The police can't ever know. My mother will never know. Promise me, Gus."

"Okay. I promise." I made a promise I knew I wouldn't keep.

I picked her up and carried her to her room. I placed her under the sheets of her bed and sat next to her and held her hand all night. She cried out in her sleep and sometimes woke up crying. Each time, I wiped the tears from her face, being careful around her bruised eye, and each time she fell asleep again. She never let go of my hand and I never slept. I stared out the window at the large oak trees in her yard and thought of ways to kill the lawyer. I planned how I would catch him off guard and hang him, or castrate him, or humiliate him in public. I thought of violent ways to destroy the man that had just destroyed my girl next door.

Chapter 20

Ogie borrowed his parents' Suburban SUV for the night and was driving as I sat in the passenger seat and told him, Cassady, and Darwin what had happened to Yonah.

None of them spoke until I prompted, asking, "What would you do?"

"I'd kill the son of a bitch. I'd kill him," Cassady said. "Let's go find him right now and hang him."

"No, we don't have to do that. We can tell my dad," Darwin responded.

"We can't do that. I mentioned that to her. She said no way. We can't tell the police. I shouldn't be telling y'all, but I don't know what else to do."

"I already told you what to do," Cassady reminded me.

"I heard what you said and, believe me, I want to kill him, but I don't want to spend the next twenty years in jail either."

"Not even for Yonah? Would you kill someone that hurt me?" Darwin asked.

"I don't know," I said. I felt guilty for not wanting to kill, for not being capable of killing. "You're right, Darwin. I know you are. I guess we have to do something. I just don't know what that something is. I've never been so confused and without answers. I wish my dad was here. I need him."

The vehicle was quiet. Darwin had made a good point and I knew it. A girl I loved, a person that was one of my best friends, a person that had taught me what a friend is had been hurt, hurt terribly, by an evil person. Elly's words that night months ago now made more sense than ever. What can you do when you can't turn to the police or to a parent, but justice has to be done? I was angry with Darwin for asking the question I was already asking myself. I was angry at myself for not knowing what to do, or at the least for not doing what I wanted to do, for not having the guts to do what my soul told me to do, but my heart wouldn't let me do—kill.

I was returned from my thoughts by the pounding of Ogie's fist against the dashboard. He was driving with one hand and hitting with the other, while at the same time pushing down on the accelerator causing the Suburban to go faster and faster. The back road was empty and straight and before Ogie stopped hitting the dashboard we were going over 90 miles per hour.

"I can't believe it. I can't believe that sorry sack of shit did it. What if...what if it was Kendi? Every one of us cares about her and as the S.S.D. we have an obligation to do something. We have an obligation to her as human beings. We can't let this go. We can't ignore this. Dammit, Gus. This can't be ignored."

Darwin reached from the backseat and put his hand on Ogie's shoulder. "Ogie, slow down man. I know you're mad, but we can't help her if we're dead." Ogie took his foot of the pedal and we coasted as Darwin continued. "We can't kill him. We are not killers. It's not who we are."

"Speak for yourself," Cassady said. "I'll kill him. Drop me off at his house right now and I'll blow his fucking brains out. No. I'll torture him first. Then I'll tie him to a chair and burn his house down."

"I'm mad too, Cassady," Darwin said. "But you're not a killer, even if you want to kill. None of us are. We are the S.S.D. and we'll figure something out, but we don't kill or torture people. We can royally screw his life up without killing him."

"How, how do we do that, Darwin?" I asked.

"I don't know yet. We'll figure it out. We won't let him get away with this, but we need to be patient. Something will come up. It always does. It's karma you know. Karma will take care of this. Something will happen to him. Karma will get him back."

Two hours later, we were all drunk. Ogie had stolen a bottle of Jack Daniels from his father's liquor cabinet and we had finished it.

I usually drank very little liquor, but my soul was sad and the elixir was the only thing I'd found so far to soothe it. Cassady had thrown up out the window and the vehicle smelled of vomit, sweat and alcohol. Darwin was sleeping next to Cassady, who had vomit on his pants that he didn't notice in his stupor. When I say we were all drunk, I suppose we all were, but it was difficult to know how drunk Ogie was. Maybe it was his proper upbringing, or maybe just his mass, but it always took much more to reduce him, and even though he had consumed more than Cassady, Darwin, and me combined, he acted sober, even though he said he was "blasted out of his mind."

"Boys, wake up. Cassady, Darwin wake up. Look over there." Ogie slowed down and pulled into the parking lot of the Hoot Owl Lounge, a dive bar in a rectangular building just across the Caswell County line that was known for serving to underage kids. "Gus, do you recognize those three white trash assholes standing next to that truck?"

I did. It was the three rednecks we had fought in the movie theatre the weekend before. "I guess we won't be drinking in there tonight. Those boys probably have a dozen friends in that joint," I said.

"I guess we won't," Ogie said. "But that doesn't mean we can't mess with them some. I'm pretty damn pissed tonight and those assholes are in the wrong place at the wrong time." Ogie put the Suburban in park, but left the engine running.

"Are you sure those are the guys y'all fought with in the movie theatre?" Darwin asked, pointing to the three men leaning against a jacked-up pick-up truck. The truck was painted bright red and had two Confederate flags on poles hooked to the bed of the truck. The tires were oversized, giving the truck over two feet of clearance from the ground.

"Yeah, that's them," I said. "And Ogie, I think we settled with them. You threw one of them into a movie screen—during a movie I'd like to add."

"I know, but I want to break something tonight. I want to screw with somebody that deserves it. Isn't that what the S.S.D. does? We screw with those that deserve it."

Darwin's hand shook when he said, "Ogie, I have to go with Gus on this. They're ain't no reason to start another fight. And besides, they probably have a bunch of friends in that bar that would love to beat a few high school kids senseless just for fun."

"We don't have to fight 'em," Cassady said. We thought he was passed out.

"Cassady, nice to have you back among the living. What are you talking about?" I asked.

"We don't have to get in a fight. Just wait for them to go back into the bar."

"Then what?" Ogie asked.

"We torch their truck. They deserve it for disgracing the Confederate battle flag."

"Look. They're going in," Darwin noticed. "Talk about timing, Cass."

"See, that didn't take long." Cassady smiled and a chunk of dried vomit fell from his lips.

"Alright, now what Cassady?" Ogie asked before putting his hand over his mouth to defend his nose against the smell.

Cassady opened the door and fell to ground. I got out quickly to help him, but he was already back on his feet. He pushed past me and reached into the dashboard of the Suburban and took out a large hunting knife. Cassady then took an old t-shirt from the backseat floor and wiped the vomit from his face. We watched as he first cut the Confederate battle flags from the poles attached to the jacked-up pick-up truck. He ran back and handed me the flags. Then he ran back to the truck.

"What's he going to do now?" I asked.

"I don't know but it looks like fun. I'm going to help," Ogie said.

I stood on the running boards of the Suburban so I could get a better look at what Ogie and Cassady were doing and also so I could see any cars coming down the road or anyone leaving the bar. The music inside was loud and each time the door opened, the music grew louder, making it easier to observe anyone coming outside.

Cassady went to each tire and cut the valve stems. This would have been a major inconvenience and more than enough to satisfy any lingering hostilities I had toward the men, but Ogie was always one that went the extra mile and when I saw him take the t-shirt from Cassady and stuff it into the gas tank I knew the night was about to get interesting.

"They're not…they're not going to blow up that truck are they?" Darwin asked.

"Man, I don't know. Yeah, yeah I think I do know. Yeah, they're going to blow up that truck. Oh shit!"

I expected to see Ogie light the cotton t-shirt that was now soaked in gas and hanging from the gas tank, but instead he pulled it out of the tank, opened the door to the pick-up truck, and tossed the soaked shirt inside. Then Cassady reached in and pushed the cigarette lighter in the truck. When it popped he removed it and tossed it on the shirt.

"Whatch y'all doin'," asked a familiar voice I couldn't immediately place. I was transfixed on the truck and forgot to watch for people. I jumped from the running board and turned quickly to see Sergeant Dusty Raines from the state militia. "Looks like you soldiers are takin' care of some business tonight."

"Yes, Sergeant. We are, they are, uh, we are I guess," I said stumbling over my words. "Where did you come from? I didn't see you." My heart pounded like an overworked water pump. We were caught and jail was the only possible outcome I could predict at that moment.

"I was pissing around back. The bathroom inside was locked." The militia sergeant brushed his hand through his greasy hair and said, "Know what? I hate those sons 'o bitches." Dusty smiled. "Meanest boys around. There's no need for Klan. Ain't no need to be that mean. Those son a bitches ripped me off in a game of pool to top it off. You go right ahead and do what needs to be done. In fact, I saw a red corvette pull out of the parking lot and it went in the opposite direction you're gonna go. You get my drift?"

"We sure do Sergeant. Thank you," Darwin said looking over his shoulder as Ogie and Cassady ran back to us, illuminated by the flames from the cab of the truck.

We all jumped into the Suburban and pulled slowly out of the gravel parking lot of the bar and onto the road. Behind us, flames grew larger inside the pick-up truck. Ogie was smiling as we picked up speed and the flames grew dim in the distance. His grudge with the rednecks was settled.

Cassady held up the flags and said, "The Klan stole these flags from the Confederacy. We just stole them back."

Chapter 21

"Judge Rush will see you now," the young, blond secretary told me. I was nervous and I knew what I was doing could cause great pain for me and my family and could be detrimental to Yonah, maybe even landing her in a foster home or orphanage, but I saw no other options for dealing with Taft Gregory.

The secretary answered the phone when I opened the door to the judge's office on the first floor of the court house. The brass doorknob was so cold it sent a shock to my heart—or maybe it was nerves. The judge's office was lined, from the navy blue carpeted floor to the copper tiled ceiling, with dark stained wood. On the wall behind his desk were several degrees and a picture of him standing next to Jimmy Carter.

The old judge looked up at me and smiled. "Mr. Ambrose, is it? Augustus Ambrose. Your brother's the musician? Is that right?"

"Yes sir, yes sir that's me, and he's my brother."

"I heard him play at the municipal theatre last summer. He's quite a talent. What's he doing now?"

"He's preparing for a European tour right now sir. I think he's in New York City this week practicing with a small orchestra."

"My my. That is impressive. So, do you play anything? What is your talent?"

"I uh, I don't play anything sir. My little brother is the prodigy. I'm just an average teenager."

The judge laughed.

"Well, I guess you're staying out of trouble?" He winked. "Now what can I do for you today?"

"Well sir, your honor, this isn't easy to say. I have something bad to tell you, but um…"

"It's okay son. You can talk to me. I've been doing this job for a long time and have heard just about everything."

"Yes sir. Thank you. Well, I'm here today to talk about Yonah Cook. You know, Dr. Cook's daughter."

"Yes, I know them well. Very sad. Very sad situation."

"Yes your honor it is. Well it just got worse. For Yonah anyway. You know Mr. Gregory? The lawyer?"

"Yes, I do. Is she complaining about him again?" The judge's face grew stern.

"No sir, she didn't want me to come here at all. She doesn't know about this meeting." I fidgeted.

"Go on son."

"Sir, your honor, Mr. Gregory attacked her. He raped her." There it was. I said it out loud to someone I didn't know. The words didn't feel like my own. The judge stared at me and I felt I needed to say more so I continued. "She confronted him about stealing from her mother's account so he beat her up and raped her." It was such a simple sentence for such a violent act.

The judge stood up, put his hands on his desk and leaned toward me. "Son, you don't know what you're saying. You're swimming in a dangerous swamp. Boy, you better get your head on straight." The judge's face was turning red and his stare was so damaging I looked down. I couldn't help but notice his pants were unzipped. Instantly I was two people: a teenager wanting to laugh at the old man that couldn't remember to zip his pants and an adult dealing with corruption and violence.

"Your honor, I saw her the night he did it. I saw her busted eye and bloody nose. I saw her cry. I saw her weep. You weren't there, but I was."

"Damn right I wasn't there because it didn't happen. If it did, all she had to do was call the police and they would have called me. There's a process for this, son. You can't go around making accusations that ain't true. You just can't do it. You ever heard of slander? You keep it up and everything your family has worked for can be taken away. Taft can sue you for making up stuff like this about him."

I felt myself growing angry. I wanted to slap the old man and grab him by his collar and shake sense into him. Why didn't he believe me? Why was he refusing to believe? Why was he threatening me? Wasn't he here to help, to serve those weaker than him? "Have you ever audited Dr. Cook's accounts? I will bet something is wrong. I'll bet money has been stolen. If not, then Mr. Gregory would have been happy to have an audit to clear up any questions." I hated calling the lawyer "Mr.," but I wanted the judge to listen and thought the faux respect might keep him from dismissing my arguments. The "Mr." was nothing more than a title and no respect was inferred.

The judge stood up and walked around his desk. He was as mad as anyone I had ever seen and I expected him to swing at me, so I stood up, expecting a physical fight. It was apparent to me now that we both wanted to end this like men…with our fists. Instead, we contained our anger as instructed by the modern societal norms that both of us wanted to break. The judge put his face so close to mine, I could smell rank coffee breath as he spoke. His voice trembled like someone riding a bicycle over a bumpy gravel road.

"Taft is a good man. You don't know him and his family like I do. Just last month he gave five thousand dollars to Middle Baptist Church so they could send some teenagers to Africa to build a church for them poor colored folks over there. Now, would a man like that do what you just described? Ain't nothing gonna happen to that fine young lawyer. You keep this up and I'll make your life a living hell. You ain't nothing but a white trash trouble maker. Now get outa my office."

I calmed. I knew the judge was powerful. I knew I was questioning the integrity of a corrupt political system. I knew I was trying to knock down a brick wall with a plastic sledgehammer, and there was little I could do to change anything. But I also knew I was on the side of right. I could see death in Judge Rush's face and his demise strengthened me. His days were numbered and when he died, change would come. I knew there was little I could do at seventeen, but I also knew I would someday grow into an adult that wouldn't stand for cronyism. With every death, retirement and election the South was changing for the better.

I had no intention of going to the police, but I wanted to shake the nerves of the judge once more before I left. I wanted to push him closer to the coffin. "Your honor, if you won't do the job the good people of Caswell County elected you to do that's fine. Your time is short anyway." I smiled and took more control from the judge. "I know the sheriff well. I'm good friends with his son. You probably know Darwin. Anyway, the sheriff is a man of integrity, unlike you."

The judge clenched his fist and bit down so hard his lips puckered. He spoke. "I'll tell you this son. Even if you tell your friend's daddy about this and Taft gets arrested it won't matter. I know every judge and every D.A. for a hundred miles. I have a lifetime of favors built up. Even if he gets arrested, it won't do any good." The judge unclenched his fist and pointed his finger in my face. "If Taft gets arrested or any stink is made about this, I promise you that little girl's going to learn what public embarrassment is. Her mother will get to see it too, boy. That little girl won't be the same after a trial and she'll spend the next year in the most expensive orphanage I can find." The judge poked his finger in my chest as he said, "I can promise you that." He had taken control of the fight again, but his words showed me that his ego was another one of his weaknesses. "Don't ever forget that I'm in control and what I say goes. The probate is mine and mine alone and what I say in this court and this town is law."

I walked to the door and grabbed the cold, brass door knob. I wanted to run, but forced myself to remain composed so I could leave the judge with my final thought before leaving. I turned and said, "Judge Rush. You're too old to be this evil. How many years do you think you have left? How many days? I bet it's just days. Shouldn't you be getting your karma in place for what's next? Are you really going to let this happen? You know, you're no better than the man that did this? The world you have fought to protect is dying, just like you, and when you are gone, it will all change. With you in Hell, the South will take one step closer to the Heaven I know it can be."

I turned, opened the door and walked past the secretary and into the marble and oak lined grand hallway of the courthouse. The judge was yelling at me. I heard him say something about being saved by Jesus and karma and somewhere he used the word shit. I had never heard anyone use that four-letter word in the same sentence as 'being saved by Jesus.' When religion and profanity merge, you know you've done something right.

Chapter 22

Moonlight reflected off the water and illuminated the mist rising from swamp. The small wooden boat I sat in moved slowly. Even though I didn't have a watch, I knew it was the moment before midnight. On the bank, three white flowers pushed through the mud and contrasted with the dark mulch of the ground and the night. I jumped when I heard a clock begin to chime. It was the courthouse bell from downtown. The noise startled me, but I wasn't surprised to hear it so far away from town. I should have been.

As the last chime faded, the wind picked up and rain hit the water, diminishing the mist. Suddenly, rain became fire that burned my skin, but I didn't try to escape. Flesh fell from my body and hit the wooden floor of the boat like raw cookie dough and I screamed, but stopped when I realized there was no pain. The drops of fire from the sky grew larger and less frequent, but now more devastating. Flaming spheres the size of basketballs hit the ground in the woods next to the swamp and Cypress trees burst into flames. The woods glowed red. The fire balls grew even less frequent, but again larger. A sphere as large as a car slammed into the swamp, creating a wave that threw me from the boat. My feet didn't find the bottom of the swamp and I was pulled down like a bug in a drain. I fought my way to the surface, and finally to shore, through the swirling waves.

I looked down at the three flowers that were now scorched black, but still standing. I touched one flower, but it turned to dust and blew away. The fire grew, sucking the oxygen from the air. I pulled in hard with my lungs and stood to run before a large cypress tree fell and blocked my path. I turned to go the other way and another tree fell. I considered going back into the swamp when it suddenly came alive with water moccasins. They floated on the waves and opened their mouths, revealing their white, cotton mouths and fangs. I looked up to see a red sky. I knew I was going to die.

The red glow slowly shrank and blackness surrounded me. The fire was gone, the water was gone. I found myself lying on the floor, in the center of a pentagram, in Mother Elly's rental house where I had experienced the shared vision. I tried to stand, but couldn't. My body was numb and my muscles useless. The pentagram somehow held me down. A group of shadowy figures in black robes surrounded me before two pulled back their hoods. I recognized Judge Rush and Taft Gregory, the attorney that raped Yonah. Gregory raised a knife above his head and swiftly swung the knife back down and into my heart. I tried to scream, but my voice was silent.

I awoke in a cold sweat. It was 12:05 AM. I cried, no, I wept. I was alone, cold and I missed my family. I needed my family.

Chapter 23

"What is this?" I asked, leaning toward my car dashboard. Darwin had put a new cassette tape into my radio.

"It's the Black Crowes. They're a new band."

"Turn it down," Cassady yelled from the back. It was odd that he wanted the radio turned down. Usually he was turning it up.

"Something up, man? Why don't you want to hear the radio?" Ogie asked from the backseat, next to Cassady.

"I don't mind the music. It's a good band. I guess I have a lot on my mind," Cassady responded.

"Like what? You never worry about anything," I said.

"I don't know. It's just that graduation is coming in a few months and I still don't know what I want to do. Ogie has his entire life planned out and I don't even know what I'm doing a year from now, even a few months from now. I told my parents I submitted applications to colleges, but I didn't. If I was excited about anything, I might feel better, but I don't know what I want to do. And then there's this craziness with Yonah that has my head all messed up. I wish things were simple."

"Look man, you don't have to know right now," I said. "Just enroll and starting taking core classes. You don't have to make up your mind already. It'll be a couple of years before you start taking your major classes anyway. You have time. And this stuff with Yonah, well, I don't know what we can do, but we can't stop living."

"Yeah, you're right about Yonah, but it still has me torn up inside. I agree with you about college, or at least I know what you're saying. I do, but I'm not even sure if college is for me."

"Are you talking about the military?" Darwin asked.

"No. Not at all. I don't want to join the Army, or the Navy, or go to college and I don't even want to get a job."

"I don't want a job either, Cassady. That's why I'm going to college," I said and looked back at him and smiled, hoping to lighten his mood.

"That's funny, Gus."

"And it's true," Ogie agreed. "At least y'all have options. If I wanted to join the military it would be fine, but I'd still be expected to come back and run the family company. One Oglethorpe man or another has kept my family prosperous for over two centuries. I don't have a choice. Cassady, you think not knowing what you want to do is bad, try not having a choice. Sure, I can do anything I want in the short term as long as the end is me coming back to River Falls and doing what my father has done and all my grandfathers since the creation of the great state of Georgia."

"That does suck. Sorry I brought it up," Cassady said. "You have it much worse." Cassady smiled.

Ogie gave Cassady a dirty look and then continued. "And guess what the best part is. If I fail, I'll be the first Oglethorpe man in recorded history to fail. No one in my family fails. The stress of it gives me a headache. I don't want to think about it, but I have to think about it."

"No one cares what I do," I said. "My little brother takes up so much of my parent's time, they don't care what I do. At all." I stopped myself for a moment. "That's not true. They do care. It's just that this is a once in a million opportunity for my little brother—for all of us. My family, unlike Ogie's, has never gotten anything right. Now my brother is making up for years and years of pain and poverty. My parents worked hard so that everything in the future could be better. My brother is living the dream they created. I feel like as asshole complaining, but it still pisses me off. I could really use my parents sometimes. Especially right now."

"It's okay to complain, Gus," Darwin said. "Think about it. Your parents and brother are gone for months of the year. I don't think I could be so mature if my parents were never home. I'd probably have a party every night and then cry myself to sleep when everyone went home. And yes, you are an asshole, but not for being upset about your family."

"Man, don't listen to Darwin—even with your parents around you're not mature," Cassady joked.

"Hey, speaking of parents, Ogie. When are you going to tell your parents about Kendi?" I asked, looking over my shoulder.

For a few seconds the only sound was the music from the radio. Then Ogie answered. "Soon. I don't know when. I've been planning on telling them, but I haven't been able to do it."

Darwin turned around and faced Ogie. "Look, brother. She's a great person. One of the best people I know. Your parents will love her. They already know her because she comes to your house to study." Darwin made air quotes when he said study. "In fact, they probably already love her. I don't think they'll be upset. I don't. I'm not sure why, but I really believe they'll be okay with it."

"Y'all don't know the world I live in. My family owned slaves. I've never once heard my father say anything that leads me to believe he regrets that. He doesn't disparage blacks, but I haven't seen any regret either."

"Why should he regret something he didn't do?" Darwin said. "And you know, that's a really long time ago."

"Well, I regret it," Ogie said, "And apparently it hasn't been long enough. Just look at my church."

"What do you mean?" Darwin asked.

"At church, we're told to be like Christ, but the people telling me these things are hypocrites. They are scared and angry elitists. They say to love your brother, but they mean to only love him from a distance. Their idea of Christianity is sending money to African kids while ignoring poor black kids a mile from their own homes."

"I'm so glad I don't go to church," Cassady mumbled from the backseat.

"Do you even believe in God?" Darwin asked Cassady.

"I believe in God when I need him."

Cassady's comment frustrated Darwin who responded, "It's not God that's the problem, Cass. It's the churches."

"What about Elena? She's pretty religious. She's a hard core Catholic. You don't get much more religious than that," I said.

"She loves her religion. No doubt about it," Darwin said to me. "But it's more than that. She has faith. True faith. It's just another thing that makes her special. You know, we talk about sex with girls a lot. And I love it. Don't get me wrong, but there's more. Elena wants to wait till she's married and I'm willing to wait."

"What the…" Ogie reached up and slapped Darwin on the head.

"Ouch. What was that for?" Darwin asked.

"What are you talking about man? Are you saying you want to marry her?"

"Yes gentleman, that's what I'm saying. I love her in ways I didn't know were possible. If she wants to wait, I'll wait. Even if that means waiting for four more years until we finish college to get married."

"Damn, marrying a virgin. I've only read about that in fairy tales," Cassady said and we all laughed.

Chapter 24

When the Black Crowes tape ended, we turned on the radio and learned a tornado was ripping through the northern part of Caswell County. We were fifteen miles away, but the excitement of a storm was too much for us to ignore, so we drove to Highway 85 and headed toward the location of the last touch-down.

We burst through a wall of rain and were in the middle of the storm. Pollen season in Georgia had started and everything was coated yellow, but the rain promised to wash away the pollen—at least for a day. First, the rain caused the yellow to streak over the windshield and then washed it from the car as the water became so heavy I feared it would drown us. The side of the highway was now a yellow river as the bright dust mixed with the new rain like mud being washed from a dirty child.

Tornados, snowstorms and other odd weather phenomenon in Caswell County were common in the spring, thanks to a combination of warm weather from the Gulf of Mexico and the occasional cold front that dipped from the north. Caswell County was right on the line between the two contrasting air systems that twisted together to create violent and memorable storms. My earliest memories of life and my first memories of school included huddling in the safest area of the house or school building while winds thumped the doors and windows like a monster looking for children to devour. Thanks to the seriousness of the drills and the shrillness of storms, even a wind would cause classmates to breakout in crying fits of terror. Somehow I didn't share their fear of storms and even enjoyed them, like the one we were currently chasing.

The roads were clear of cars as we headed north on Highway 85, the quickest route to the north end of the county, but the highway patrol had the highway closed before the last exit in the county. That was fine with us, as the exit let us off in the area of the most damage. Usually, storms moved in and out fast and we expected the storm to be gone when we arrived, but it was still beating the ground and twisting the trees like paper bags when we exited near a trailer park that had lost trailers an hour before, and from the looks of the storm, was going to lose a few more.

I took a left at the top of the ramp and crossed the bridge over the highway. Half-way across, a wind hit the side of my Mustang like a stampeding elephant and sent us into the other lane. I tried to correct against the wind and overcompensated, causing the car to fish-tail and then to spin in one complete circle on the bridge. The spinning killed the engine and we were sitting in the middle of the bridge as the sound of the pounding rain muffled Darwin's screams. I couldn't tell if he was afraid or excited. I looked at Darwin and then to the backseat to see if anyone was hurt. Cassady's fingers were dug into the front seat like a mountain climber, but he was smiling. Ogie looked at me and shrugged his shoulders like I had just asked him a question.

I looked at Darwin again, who was now silent, and asked him, "Are you okay?"

"What? I can't hear you?" He yelled back to me.

"Are you okay?" I yelled in response.

"No, I'm not okay. We almost ran off a bridge and now we're sitting in the highest spot for miles in the middle of the storm of the century."

I was glad to have survived the spin. I started the Mustang's engine and drove away from the bridge toward the mobile home park. The windows were fogging up and I quickly learned that the spin broke my heat and defroster. I pointed to the dashboard in front of Darwin and said, "I don't know what's wrong with the defrost, but I'm going to need you to wipe the windows. There's a rag in the dashboard. I can't see a thing."

Darwin took an old cloth from the dashboard and wiped the windshield in front of me. Even with the fog off the windshield, I could only see a few feet in front of the car. I followed the white lines on the side of the road, driving slowly with my hazard lights blinking in rhythm.

"Wipe! Wipe the window, Darwin," I yelled as the windshield fogged up again. "You have to keep wiping. Don't stop because I can't see a thing."

"I'm wiping as fast as I can, dammit. I can't wipe any faster," Darwin said, imitating Scotty from Star Trek. I was so nervous that I didn't know why he was using the accent.

"Okay, whatever. Just wipe. Wipe the windows."

Darwin wiped the windows every few seconds as they fogged up. We drove several miles past the bridge and I took a right on a road I thought lead to the trailer park, but this was a wrong turn followed by another wrong turn that soon put us in a place none of us recognized. We were in an unfamiliar area in the middle of a storm. The windows were fogged and the rain was so heavy that I could only see a few feet past the front bumper.

"We should just backtrack. Retrace our steps," Cassady suggested from the backseat. I agreed and tried to pull into the first driveway we had seen in several minutes, but the car was moving too fast and we hydroplaned over water and started spinning again, as we had on the bridge, but this time the spins kept coming. With each spin, the tires screamed into the black and wet night like a bobcat in heat. I lost count of the spins and lost complete control of the car as the momentum and wind pushed the car into chaos. Finally, the blur ended and the car stopped. We were now sitting perfectly aligned in the driveway in front of a ranch style house. The power was out in the house and if anyone was home, they didn't come out. The screaming tires may have sounded like another part of the damaging storm to the inhabitants, or maybe, scared them into remaining still in their hallway.

"I'm not driving any more. We can sit it out right here or we can see if anyone will help us at that house," I said.

"I don't want to go into anyone's house way out here," Darwin said. "We don't know who lives there. Anyway, who's going to let four teenage boys into their house on a night like this?"

The storm passed a few minutes later and the night cleared as quickly as a curtain being pulled back. Even though it was night, we had more light than we had had for the last hour, so we decided it was safe to leave, but two flat tires killed that plan. I knocked on the door of the ranch house, but, as suspected, no one was home.

"We're going to have to walk, boys. I only have one spare tire," I told the others.

"There's no need for all of us to walk," Darwin said.

"I ain't walking while you sit here and sleep, and your dad is probably the only one awake right now. You can call him to send someone to get us."

"Alright, then. Let's all go. A night walk never hurt anyone," Darwin stated. "How far are we from the exit?"

"A few miles," I said. "I hope I can remember how to get back to the exit. I got turned around in the storm."

"Yes, you did get turned around in the storm. As I remember you turned around and around and around. You're lucky I didn't puke in your car," Cassady said.

"It was the storm."

"Yeah, the storm you drove way too fast through."

"Would you have been happier if I poked through it?" I asked.

"No, now that I think of it, I guess the spinning was fun."

We began walking.

We walked for several miles with no words. The sound of water from the heavy rain rushed by in the ditches next to the road and the power lines above the ditches that were still charged buzzed with static providing a chorus of sounds. After reaching a road we recognized, we started on the last leg to the highway and a gas station that we hoped would have a pay phone.

"I love the dark," Ogie said as a wind twisted the pines making them crack and sing. "It's most quiet at night. I love being alone in the woods when no one else is around. Sometimes I sing to myself."

"What do you sing?" Darwin asked.

"Simon and Garfunkel." Ogie closed his eyes for a moment and then slowly quoted, almost sang, the words to "Sound of Silence."

He finished the song and breathed deeply. Ogie had just shared something deeply personal with us and we could not respond, as there was no response appropriate. All we could do was listen with our hearts and make what we could of his prophecy. In that moment, he revealed his soul to us while at the same time showing us that he was beyond our ability to comprehend.

Darwin smiled to let us know the pay phone at the old gas station was working when he called the sheriff's office to contact his father, who we were sure was working late due to the storm. We could all hear Sheriff Mayflower cussing when he was connected with Darwin who kept saying, "yes sir, yes sir" in response to his father's lecture.

I couldn't hear what the sheriff said before Darwin asked, "Do you know where she is now? Did she come home yet?" Then Darwin told his father where we were.

When he hung up the phone, he looked nervous. "Elena went looking for us. She's missing and hasn't come home yet. It's 1:00 AM now. Her mother keeps calling my dad and he has everyone looking for her…and us."

"What do you mean she's missing?" I asked.

"She's missing. I don't know what it means." Darwin was shaking his head and pacing. "My dad is sending a car to pick us up."

Twenty minutes later, a sheriff's car from Clayton County pulled into the parking lot of the gas station. We hadn't realized that the exit was right on the county line. The officer stopped near us and was talking on the radio when Darwin started walking toward the car.

"Where are you going?" Cassady asked.

"I'm getting a ride. This is for us."

"Are you sure?" Cassady asked.

"Yes, I'm sure. Why else would he be here?" Darwin said as he opened the back door of the Clayton County Deputy Sheriff's car and sat in the back seat and closed the door. The officer jumped out of his car and put his hand on his gun.

"What the hell are you doing in my car?" The officer yelled.

Cassady was right. This was not the car we were waiting for. When the officer started yelling, Darwin realized it too.

"Get out of my car, you stupid punk. Get out of my damned car right now."

Darwin fumbled with the inside of the door, but there was no handle and no way out of the back of the car. Darwin's eyes grew wide with fear. "I can't get out. There's no way out."

"Boy, I don't know who you think you are, but you don't go gettin' in my car for no damn good reason. I think I might take you to jail." The deputy looked back at us to ensure we were not a threat, but he kept his hand on his gun. "Why are you out here in the middle of the night?" I started to answer and he cut me off. "Never mind. I don't wanna know."

I thought we were all going to jail when a Caswell County sheriff's car pulled into the parking lot and saved us. The Caswell County deputy stepped out of his car and the two deputies approached each other and talked for a minute. The deputy that had arrived to pick us up started laughing.

"Alright, boys. I guess I came at a good time. You boys were about thirty seconds from getting free room and board for the night," the Caswell County deputy said to us as he opened the door of his colleague's car to free Darwin. "You're lucky your dad is sheriff, Darwin. You get in about as much trouble as your mamma."

It was 3:00 AM before I finally made it to bed. I was lucky my parents were away in another city, but my friends would be meeting their parents and suffering the wrath of coming home well beyond curfew. Most of the time I missed my parents, but on that night I was glad they were gone.

Chapter 25

My hair was still wet from my morning shower when I noticed the light blinking on the answering machine. At first, it made me nervous because I thought my parents had found out I was out most of the night, but it was much worse.

"Elena is dead. Call me." Darwin's voice on the machine was dry, but not sad. It wasn't the voice of someone who had just lost the first love of his life. It wasn't the voice of someone that had learned the girl he wanted to marry was dead. It was something else I didn't recognize. My hand shook as I picked up the phone, but then returned it to the receiver. What was I going to say? How was I supposed to deal with this? How was I going to comfort my best friend? I wasn't sad about Elena. I wasn't anything. I was numb. These things take time to set in I told myself.

I built up my courage and called Darwin's house. His mother answered the phone. "Mrs. Mayflower, this is Gus. Is Darwin there?"

"No, Gus. He's headed your way."

"Okay, I'll wait for him," I told her.

"Good. He's going to need his friends right now. You're all going to need each other." I heard what I thought was a cough, but then realized it was the physical holding back of emotion from Mrs. Mayflower. "My god, she was a good girl. We loved her to death." I heard her breath. "Well, that came out wrong. You know what I mean, don't you Gus?"

"Yes ma'am. I do. I don't know what I'm going to say to Darwin."

"You don't have to say anything. You just have to be his friend. It's going to be tough for him. It's going to be tough for all of you. This isn't a time for male toughness."

"Yes ma'am."

"And Gus?"

"Yes ma'am?"

"You come over here and talk to us if you need it. I know your parents are away and you're not as old as you think. Everyone needs someone, especially young men. Even if they don't think so."

I went to the front porch, sat on the swing and waited for Darwin. I didn't get up to meet him when he arrived in his Volkswagen van and he didn't notice my lack of manners when he walked up the steps to the porch. Darwin sat down beside me and we sat quietly for several moments before he began talking.

"Will you go with me to her house to see her parents?"

"Sure."

"It's my fault, you know."

"What's your fault?"

"Her getting killed."

I still didn't know what had happened. "I don't understand Darwin. How'd she die?"

Darwin looked away from me toward the street and he focused on something on the other side. "She went looking for us last night when we didn't come home during the tornado. She thought she knew where we might be. She was going to Gethsemane Gardens. We weren't there, of course, but she didn't know that. A tree had fallen in the road and she hit it at full speed. She was thrown out of the car and killed."

My head swam with tunnel vision. At that moment, guilt overtook me. I felt like I was the one that was driving the car. I needed to cry, but couldn't.

"I'm sorry." I searched my brain and heart for the right thing to say. "It's not your fault. You didn't know she'd come after you. We didn't know we were going to get stuck. It's not our fault. It's not anyone's fault." I lied when I told him it wasn't our fault, because I believed it was.

More time with no words passed, then Darwin spoke again. "She'll never grow old, you know. We might, but she'll always be young. She'll always be the perfect teenage girl she was the last time I saw her." Darwin looked at me. "Come with me to her house? I need to see her parents. I need to tell them I'm sorry."

Of all things in the world I wanted to do least that day was to see Elena's parents, but I felt responsible and believed I deserved whatever punishment her parents bestowed on us, so I drove Darwin to her house. We drove past her parent's restaurant and noticed a sign on the door. It was easy to guess how the sign read. When we arrived at her house, a dozen cars were parked on the road. Her father was in the yard and I saw the same lack of emotion on his face that I had seen on Darwin's. I guessed that it was caused when a vacuum is left when someone loved greatly is taken.

The walk from Darwin's van to Elena's father was no more than a hundred feet, but it felt like a mile uphill. My breathing sped up and my heart thumped erratically. I stepped onto the property and felt like a death row inmate walking his final steps in front of a leering audience as I felt the eyes of family and close friends upon us.

Did they know who we were? Did they blame us? Elena's brother was in the yard, but he walked inside when he saw us. If he had returned with a gun I wouldn't have been surprised. The walls of the small brick house were not thick enough to mask the screams of Señora Luna and I cringed when she shrieked. "What have we done?" I thought.

Darwin faced Señor Luna and then dropped to his knees. He folded forward and grabbed the legs of his dead girlfriend's father.

Darwin begged for forgiveness. "I'm so sorry. I'm so, so sorry. I love her. I loved her. Please forgive me. I didn't know. I just didn't know."

Señor Luna looked to the sky and said something in Spanish, I presume to God, before looking down at my friend. Luna touched the head of Darwin, then fell like a mighty oak next to Darwin and grabbed him. I thought he was going to shake Darwin or throw him out of his yard, but, instead, he held him tight and embraced him with love usually reserved for one's child. "It was an accident, Niño, only an accident. We do not know why God has done this. I do not know why," he said with his thick accent.

Darwin placed his head against the man's chest, his eyes closed. I stood still, paralyzed by the moment, not knowing what to do as I witnessed the act of forgiveness. Señor Luna loved his daughter more than could be articulated in any language and that love was so strong that he passed that love in his embrace to the boy she had died for.

Elena's brother exited the house and the creaking screen door ended the moment between Darwin and Señor Luna. He held open the door so Elena's dog, Misty, could leave. She exited and walked to Luna and Darwin. Misty whimpered and then began licking the tears from Señor Luna's face. He laughed through his tears and hugged the mixed golden retriever. "Hola perro," he said. "Elena loved this dog. She found her at a trash dump when she was still a puppy," Señor Luna said as he petted the dark red fur of the animal. He thought about something for a moment and then said, "Will you take her? Elena loved Misty. I have seen you play with Misty many times when you were waiting on Elena to get ready for your dates. I know Misty likes you as she did Elena."

"But she's your family dog. I can't take her," Darwin said, shocked.

"No, you must. She will be happy with you. And…it hurts too much to see her, so please take her."

"Yes sir. I will, if it helps you; I'll take good care of her. I promise," Darwin said without any more hesitation.

I expected anger and hostility when we made our rounds through the house, but we were shown only affection. If not for us, their daughter would still be alive, but they didn't consider cause and effect. It was simply the will of God and not our fault.

I didn't believe it was God's will to take a perfect young girl and I knew nothing good would come from her death. There was still something powerful in their love that I didn't understand, but I knew it was from a power much greater than myself. We didn't need to ask for forgiveness, even though I needed it desperately. Elena had left the safety of her home to find us and had died. I couldn't understand how they forgave us and I wasn't sure I would ever be able to show that sort of forgiveness to others. I was sure of it, as I didn't share their connection to God.

We found Cassady and Ogie sitting on the front porch when we returned to my house. Darwin had called them, but after the actions of the night before, their parents were reluctant to let them go out again, especially on a school day, but after some persuading, they found their way to my house.

We all sat on the porch for at least an hour. Ogie passed a bottle of cheap wine around, but there was no laughing, no party. No words were required and even if there were, none of us had the right ones to say, so we remained silent. Occasionally, a car would drive by and we would look up or an old woman would walk down the sidewalk with her dog and would smile. On any other day, I would worry that someone in one of the cars or one of the dog walkers would tell my parents I was skipping school and drinking, but on that day I didn't care. My parents would understand, I reasoned, but even if they wouldn't understand, I didn't care.

The court house bell rang eleven times, and like a hypnotist counting backwards, the bell carried us from our mesmerized state back to reality. There are events in your life that change everything, that point you in a different direction. These are events that force you to take a new path, no matter how much you resist. This was one of those times, one of those days that would be a fork in the road that provided no option to continue on the same road as before. Moments in life are short and we had just learned this with the same revelation as Adam had after eating the forbidden fruit.

"I'm going to tell them," Ogie said as the buzz of the last bell ring faded.

"Tell who what?" I asked.

"I'm telling my parents about Kendi. Then I'm going to meet her parents. I don't care any longer who knows about us. We have a good thing. She's my first real girlfriend. She's the first girl I've ever cared about like this. I mean, what in the hell am I afraid of? We're both from good families. We're both good students. We're both going to college. We both laugh at the same jokes. We're perfect for each other. There's only one thing that makes us different and I'm tired of that."

"Good for you, man," Darwin said as he looked at Cassady and me, telling us with his eyes to agree.

"Yeah, good for you, man. I know you like her. We all like her," Cassady said, and then sat up straight.

"You know I support you, man. She's a good person and you're right that she's perfect for you," I said, "And if anyone has a problem with it, you can just throw them through a movie screen." We all laughed—the first sign of normalcy we had shared that day.

I thought about their situation and shared my thoughts with the others. "I've never considered it before you and Kendi, but now that you're with her, I'm fine with it. I guess I'm prejudiced in some ways. I don't want to be and my parents taught me not to be, but it's hard not to be. I don't know what black people think about us, but it can't be good after all the shit they've been through." I shifted my body toward Ogie.

"You know, seeing you with Kendi has changed a lot in me. Before blacks were blacks and whites were whites, whatever that means I'm not sure, but I knew we were separated. But now, Kendi is Kendi and I do know what that means. She's my friend and the girlfriend of my best friend. She's my friend before anything else and somehow that's more important than anything else."

Ogie stood up, walked to the porch railing and leaned against the rails before asking, "Will you come with me to her house later today, Gus? Will you come with me when I tell her parents about us?"

Great! Another event I would rather avoid. "Sure," I agreed.

Chapter 26

Ogie was surprised to learn that his parents accepted his relationship with Kendi.

"Do you like her?" his father asked.

"I love her," Ogie responded.

"That's enough for me, son," his father said.

Ogie's mother was more apprehensive, but she believed in the judgment of her husband and seemed to resist her fear of what others in the community would say. Why should she care? She was a leader in the community. If a leader can't change things, then why lead? Of course there would be whispers. There were always whispers. But in the past, the whispers were based on jealousy, now they would be silent rebukes. In the North, everyone says what he or she thinks, but in the South that is considered rude. Southerners will smile to your face, walk away and then talk about you behind your back. It's the polite Southern way.

Ogie left his parent's house that day proud of his name, Conrad Oglethorpe. For the first time in his life, he was proud to be among the first of Georgians. He was proud that his parents had made the state the strongest in the South and that they had adapted through the changes to remain leaders in business and the community. Now, he was leading a new change and his parents were supporting him. He expected his parents to chide him, even to banish him from his home, but he was surprised and elated by their approval of his relationship with Kendi, his girlfriend.

The conversation was simple. There was little debate. There were two reasons for this. The first is that the Oglethorpes had grown to love Kendi, as expected, during all the study sessions at their house. She was easy to love. The second reason for the easy acceptance of the relationship was that Mr. Oglethorpe had suspected that his son was in love with the girl. Before Kendi, many blacks had been in the antebellum house. There had been slaves, then servants and occasionally black tradesmen hired for maintenance and construction tasks, but Kendi was one of the first black guests that had been invited repeatedly and she had brought warmth to the house the family couldn't explain, but desired.

I drove to Kendi's house while Ogie told me the story. He couldn't believe it was so easy and was smiling more than I had ever seen him smile at one time.

"If you don't stop smiling so much, your jaw is going to hurt," I said.

"Then let it hurt. Let it hurt," he yelled.

"Now your throat is going to hurt, along with my eardrums."

The energy from the positive event with his parents had overcome the pain of Elena's death, but not the importance of sharing the relationship with Kendi's family. Life was short, even for teenagers, and now we knew it.

"How do you think they'll take it?" I asked him.

"They'll be fine with it. Probably a little surprised. Her dad knows my father. They've worked together on several deals. We're a lot alike, you know. I think Kendi's going to be surprised too. She doesn't know we're coming yet."

"Uh oh," I mumbled.

"Uh oh, what? Do you think I should've told her first?"

"Well, yeah."

He thought for a moment. "Maybe so, but it's too late now. She'll understand...I hope."

Kendi's father, Weldon Johnson, was arguably the most well known black man in Caswell County. He had played baseball for

Caswell Central, the black school before integration, leading the school to a national championship. He won an appointment to the Naval Academy and played baseball with the college before entering law school, and finally JAG, where he served until 1975, when he returned to River Falls to practice law.

Weldon Johnson could be seen dining with other lawyers – all white but him - at the barbeque restaurant outside of town at lunch on weekdays and playing golf with white judges on weekends. There was even speculation that he would someday become a judge himself, making him the county's first black judge. Johnson had broken through the barriers of race and was as successful as any other man in the county. To Ogie, and to me, we saw no reason he wouldn't be thrilled to have Ogie date his daughter.

Ogie breathed deeply and forced himself to stop fidgeting before knocking on the cherry wood door of the Johnson home. The two-story, red brick house was in a new neighborhood near the highway. The first thing I noticed about the house was the sod grass, a sure sign someone was doing well, I thought. Mrs. Johnson opened the door.

"Hello Conrad. How are you today?" She didn't wait for an answer before asking, "And who is your friend?" She looked at me with her welcoming eyes. I could see where Kendi got her looks, but resisted saying so. "Hello, I don't think we've met. I'm Kendi's mother, Mrs. Johnson"

"I'm Gus. I'm also a friend of Kendi's. We're all in school together."

"Well, come in gentlemen. I think Kendi is upstairs. Are you all working on a school project today?" She asked.

"No ma'am," Ogie stated. "I'm here to talk to you and Mr. Johnson about something."

"Who's that?" Mr. Johnson said as he walked out of his study next to the front door. The main entrance of the house lead to a large open vestibule that was open all the way to the second floor. From the second floor, one could look down over the railing. "Oh, it's Conrad. How are you doing, son? How's your father?"

"He's good, sir. I'm fine sir."

"Excellent. So what can we do for you today? Are you two selling something for school? Tell me you're raising money for the baseball team and you'll get a larger donation from me," he joked. I noticed his large Naval Academy ring that might have looked even larger if not for his giant and powerful hands. Mr. Johnson was at least six feet five inches tall and I thought that he was built more for football than baseball he was known for.

"No sir. I'm here to talk to you about Kendi."

"I don't understand. Is she in trouble? Is someone hurting her?" Johnson asked. He stood straighter, ready to defend his daughter. The idea of a threat to his daughter created a change.

"No sir. She's fine. She's okay. It's about me and her." Ogie looked at me, hoping I would finish the sentence for him. Mr. and Mrs. Johnson looked at me too and I wanted to shrink and crawl away. I looked back at Ogie and shook my head for him to tell them. "Well, you see, Mr. and Mrs. Johnson. We...uh... we're dating." The usually articulate Ogie was stumbling over his words.

Weldon Johnson's head vibrated in tiny shakes for a moment like his mind was processing too much information at once. He breathed in and became even bigger before responding to Ogie's statement.

"The hell you are," Mr. Johnson said before turning his head to the right and then back to Ogie. Mrs. Johnson grabbed her husband by the arm to control his anger and maybe to keep him from hitting Ogie. A quick cry, like the last sound of a rabbit before death, came from the top floor and we all looked to see Kendi looking down on us. Her eyes were filled with water, but she shed no tears. Ogie reached up to her and she started to reach down, but turned and walked away and past a corner out of our view.

"Conrad, I am sorry. Wait...no I'm not sorry." Weldon Johnson breathed into his large shoulders and gained more size but also composure before continuing. "It's just not going to happen, son. You and her. Well, I don't know how to say this, but you two are not the same. "

"I don't understand why you are saying this sir," Ogie said, his voice changing to that of a boy as his heart broke. "How can you deny this? We aren't hurting anyone. We like each other. In fact, we love each other. I love her anyway. I know that. So how can you do this? I thought you would understand more than anyone. I thought you'd understand."

Tears rolled down Mrs. Johnson's face. She was on Ogie's side, or at least on the side of young love. "Weldon, he's right. What are they hurting? They're just kids."

"They're not just kids," he said. "They're old enough to cause all sorts of trouble for us. I have worked too hard to build a good and safe life for this family for my daughter to blow it on one boy."

"What's wrong with him, Weldon? Can you give me one simple reason they can't date?" Mrs. Johnson asked again.

"Because he's white. Is that simple enough for you? Is that simple enough for all of you?" Mr. Weldon said it loud enough for Kendi to hear him from her room upstairs. "He's white and she's black and nothing good can ever come of this. He'll hurt her. Maybe not today, but someday. They always hurt us. They'll find a way. It's just in him. It's in the world. There ain't no way out of it." Mr. Johnson spoke louder as his grammar diminished. "Son, you ain't gonna date my daughter. Just stay away from her and get outta my house. I don't care that you think you love her because you can't. You can't love her. It just doesn't happen the way you're thinking." Mr. Johnson looked down. He was ashamed of what he had said, but he believed his words. His voice grew quiet. "Conrad, just leave. There's nothing here for you. Please go away. I know you have a good heart. I do, but it isn't enough. Just go son; just go."

Mrs. Johnson apologized as she escorted us out of her home. When the door shut we heard Kendi cry out to her mother, "Momma, Momma, why did you let daddy do that? Why didn't you stop him?" Ogie turned and reached for the doorknob but I grabbed his hand and pulled him away like a parent pulling a child from a toy store.

I opened the car door for Ogie and all but pushed him down into the passenger seat. The weight of the day was heavy on his soul and I was leading him like a soldier carrying a wounded comrade. I drove to the end of the neighborhood and pulled into the parking area near the community pool and clubhouse. A golf cart buzzed by and entered the paved golf cart trail for the neighborhood course. To end the silence, I turned on the radio. Van Morrison's song *Crazy Love* was playing. Ogie listened to the words and when the song ended said, "That's our song. We didn't have a song, but now we do. For the rest of my life, that will be our song—a song she'll never know is ours."

We sat in the car and watched golfers hit balls for another half hour before a used Volvo pulled up beside us. It was Kendi's two brothers; one was a student at River Falls High and the other a recent college graduate. Both were built like their father, but a few inches shorter. When I saw them, I was happy as I thought they were there to offer suggestions for negotiating with their father. I stepped out of the car to shake the younger brother's hand, but he slapped my hand.

"What the…what's that about?" I yelled.

"You know what it's about. You better stay away from my sister."

"I'm not hurting your sister. She's my friend."

"That's what we thought until today. You liars," the older brother responded. "Friends don't keep secrets like this."

Ogie ran around the car to assist me. I could see in his eyes his mood was not congenial.

"There you are. The boy that ruined my sister." The younger brother pointed in Ogie's face.

"Number one: Get your finger out of my face. And two: I didn't ruin your sister. I loved her. I still do."

"You did no such thing. I ain't telling you again to stay away from her."

"That's up to her, I think," Ogie responded, his voice shaking.

"Fuck you," the younger brother said to Ogie before hitting him in the jaw. The two boys were of equal height, with Ogie thinner. The hit caused Ogie's face to bounce to the left and then back, but it wasn't enough for him to stagger even slightly or to lose balance. I knew the brothers were in trouble when Ogie grabbed the attacker by the belt and collar, his signature fight move, and picked him up above his head. The younger brother was now incapable of doing anything other than flailing his arms and legs. Ogie ran toward an open trashcan at the edge of the parking lot and dumped the boy into the container, causing his legs and hands to stick out of the top like something out of a Saturday morning cartoon.

The older brother pursued Ogie only to be met with an elbow to the nose. This sent the older brother to ground, but he quickly recovered and dove after Ogie in a football move, but missed when Ogie moved to the side. This gave Ogie the opportunity to grab the legs of the older brother.

"Stop, Ogie! Don't hurt him. It won't help anything," I said as Ogie dragged his girlfriend's brother across the parking lot.

"Gus, don't make me stop. I have to do this."

"No you don't. It won't help anything."

Ogie let the older brother's legs drop to the ground. There was no more fight in the older brother, and even if there was, he now knew he could not defeat Ogie in a physical battle. Nobody could.

A crowd was now gathering on the front porch of the clubhouse, so I grabbed Ogie by the hand, as I had at Kendi's door before, dragged him to the car and pushed him again into my passenger seat. I backed my Mustang through the parking lot so that no one on the porch could read my license plate numbers. Hiding my license plate was becoming a habit. My new tires squealed as we hit the main road toward downtown.

"It's over now, forever. Even if there was a chance, it's gone now. That fight ended it," Ogie said, and I agreed with a nod. "The whole world could have been against us, but if our families had supported us…"

"I know Ogie. I'm sorry."

Ogie and Kendi had a love so pure and clean only a color-blind God could have created it. But even though God created it, the relationship wasn't strong enough to survive hundreds of years of pain and hate. God had created the love, but God also created the South and our paradise was one with rules; they had broken the rules when they crossed the invisible line and ate the forbidden fruit.

"Why did they follow us? Didn't they know to leave well enough alone?" Ogie asked.

"I don't know, man," I said as I drove down Bull Drive nearing downtown. "Their dad probably got them going."

"Yeah, maybe. It just looked like they were looking for a fight and we were easy picks."

"They were just being stupid niggers." My breath caught in my throat. I had just said the most evil word in the South. A word that was a symbol of all that was wrong, a simple word that was always there, but avoided in polite company. A word too easy to use and to hurt with.

"What?" Ogie asked looking at me with eyes that cut through my skull.

I had screwed up. There was no way out. I hated myself for saying it. For thinking it. "I know. I didn't mean it. It slipped. It just slipped." I was trying to excuse my mistake to Ogie, but mostly to myself.

"I've never heard you say that. What were you thinking?"

"I wasn't. I was mad," I responded.

"So, whenever we're mad it's okay?" Ogie's question wasn't a question, but a scold and I felt like a parent was disciplining me.

"No, it's not." I couldn't win this argument, but I wasn't trying. I deserved his rebuke.

I had never used the word in general conversation and only rarely before that. It was a point of pride. I had been raised to never say it with the same pressure as using God's name in vain. There was no room for either. I thought I was more progressive than that, but when an angry black person pushed, I pushed back with the most hurtful word in American history. I had never owned a slave, never kept anyone from sitting anywhere, never stopped anyone eating anywhere, or from drinking from any water fountain. I had gone to school with black kids and had been their friend. But now I had used the forbidden word in anger and frustration. The word would always be available to me and would always be something to establish a dividing wall between whites and blacks, between Kendi and me, between Ogie and Kendi. I hated myself for saying it and I hated the world for creating all the things that went behind the word. I hated history.

There were so few differences between us. We were more alike as Southerners than people from the north, or from another country, but there was an invisible line that everyone felt and understood that still couldn't be crossed. Everyone wanted to put the past behind, but no one could. Not the whites, not the blacks. Those that did try like Kendi and Ogie were met with suspicion and hate. They met it from those they didn't know and from those they loved.

Ogie's breathing slowed as we made a sharp left turn onto Jefferson Street and entered downtown River Falls. Large columned houses ten times our age lined the street as another reminder of places in society. I turned on my signal to turn right onto Temple Avenue toward my house when Ogie spoke again. "I get it. A few months ago I wouldn't have even responded to what you said. It would have been another dirty word like any other, but now it means more. It's really stupid, I guess. I don't know. It just matters more now when someone I care about can be hurt by it. It makes it real. That's all."

"I know. I know, Ogie. I'm sorry."

Ogie said, "You know, I think it hurts white people now as much as blacks. Whites made it stand for hate and now we're cursed with a word that will always haunt us. It will always remind us of what people can become, of what people can do to each other."

Chapter 27

I didn't sleep well the night before the funeral. It wasn't just Elena's death, but all the recent events that were preying on my soul. I had failed to protect Yonah. Even after the attack, I was useless when I tried to help her and I had watched as family and society destroyed Ogie and Kendi's relationship. When I did sleep, my dreams were so uncomfortable I wanted to wake. I dreamed of Mother Elly and Elena sitting at a table in Gethsemane Gardens. There was nothing in the dream to suggest a nightmare, but it felt uncomfortable and upset me. Another dream included Yonah being attacked, but the man wasn't the lawyer, he was an old man with translucent skin. His veins pulsated over his bony skull. Behind him, the light of a fire flickered. They were in the swamp that flowed through Gethsemane. There was nothing visual to tell me where they were, but I knew. Other terrors that night included scene after scene of evil acts throughout history. I saw tortures in the name of religion, beatings of slaves and other acts that were so clear they felt more like revelations. I saw the acts from the eyes of the victims and I saw the evil and hate in the eyes of the attackers. They say no one is truly evil, but that night I saw nothing else and it repulsed me. I learned what was possible and it scared me. I wondered if the evil I dreamed of was in me, or if it was evil attacking me.

In the morning, I was surprised to find my father in the kitchen cooking french toast. "Do you want some orange juice, son? I noticed you were out, so I walked to the store this morning and picked some up."

"Dad, you're home. I wasn't expecting you," I said as I wiped crud from the corner of my eye.

"What, you're not happy to see me?" He asked. I thought he was upset until I saw the glimmer in his eye suggesting he was kidding.

"No, I'm very happy to see you. I didn't hear you come in. Did you get here last night?"

"Yeah, I came in on a red eye. I was supposed to get in at eight last night, but there were delays. My plane didn't land until 3:00 AM."

"So, why did you come home?" I asked, but I already knew the answer.

"Elly called. She told me about your friend."

I didn't know she knew but it made sense that she did. She knew evil was running rampant. She'd predicted it. I sat at the kitchen table.

"Everyone knows, Gus. Don't forget, this is a small town," he said as he slid three pieces of french toast on a plate in front of me. He put the spatula in the frying pan and patted my back gently with his hand.

"You're right about that. I can't wait to get out of here."

"That will happen soon enough. I might as well tell you now, but we'll probably sell the house when you leave for college."

"Wow, I didn't know that." I was shocked. Usually news like this would send me spinning, but not after everything else. It seemed so small compared to the last few days.

"There's no reason to keep this house in Georgia. We are hardly here with your brother's schedule. We might buy a house in New York City. You can go to school up there if you want."

"Okay, I'll think about it. I think I'll still go to Artemas College," I said, hoping to end the discussion. I was not interested in digesting more life changing news. The week had been difficult and now it was the day of the funeral and dealing with that was enough.

"You always liked the North Georgia Mountains. Finding a school in a place you love is a great bit of luck." My father smiled and then sat down. "Talk to me, Gus. How are you doing?"

"I'm fine," I lied.

"I'm sure you are, son, but since I'm here, you can discuss anything you want with me. No pressure, but while I'm here," he said, knowing I had lied and that this was a difficult time for me.

"Thanks, Dad. It has been tough. Elena was killed and then my friends broke up—well, her parents made them break up." I didn't tell him all the details as the details didn't feel important. "This year started off like any other. It was just another year in the life of a teenager and now it's ending as the worst year of my life."

"It could get worse," he said

"Gee, thanks," I said before forcing a mock laugh. "I just don't know why it all happened. I don't know what it all means." I was unable to hide the discouragement in my voice.

"Are you looking for the secret to life? For answers?" he asked me.

"I guess. Or at least the point of it all."

"Son, the only secret is that life is painful and usually not much fun. In all, there're only a few moments of real joy, and that's what we live for. Your mother and I raised you in a sheltered world and made it as happy as we could. We tried our best to make your life better than ours, but at some point we knew you'd grow up and would have to face the things that make life hurt. Eventually, we all grow up and learn that life isn't the peachy place it's made out to be on TV."

"Yeah. I'm learning that quickly."

He closed his eyes to rest them for a moment and opened them again. This time when he looked at me, his expression was different. There was respect in his eyes I'd never seen before. "Gus, you're going to experience many new things now. You're never going to feel the things you're feeling now again. It's okay to be scared of life. You'll do fine in the long run, but I expect you'll make a few mistakes between now and then."

"When is then?" I asked.

"It's later, Gus. When you're there you'll know it and today will feel like a million years ago and yesterday all at once."

I wanted the day to end so I could start making my way toward my father's "then."

We ate breakfast together and made small talk about the town. When we finished my father asked, "So, why, uh, why did your friends break up?"

"I don't know. I mean, I mean I can't really say. It's very complicated. I don't think you'd get it."

"You'd be surprised son. I was 17 once too, you know, and not that long ago. I'm not all that different from you. I've just been putting up with shit a couple of decades longer than you and during that time I've learned a thing or two." He stood up and took our plates to the sink. "So, why did they have to break up?"

"Her parents didn't like Ogie," I said hoping that would be enough of an answer.

"How could anyone not like Ogie? He's a great kid, and any parent would love their daughter to date one of the most eligible bachelors in River Falls."

"They didn't like him because he was white."

"Huh, why would they..?" my father stopped talking when the answer came to him mid-sentence. "Oh, I see. She's not white, is she?"

"No sir. She's not. She's a black girl. Her name's Kendi Johnson. Her dad's the lawyer."

"Yes, yes I know of him. He played baseball. Pretty good from what I remember."

"Yes sir, that's him."

My father turned and looked out the kitchen window. It was so long before he spoke again I thought the conversation was over. "Son, the world is changing, but it hasn't changed enough." He turned to me. "I forget how it is down here when we're in New York or someplace like San Francisco, but down here there're still a lot of scars. A lot of pain. Mr. Johnson was wrong, but you have to understand were he's coming from. He can't forget everything that's been done to him just like that. He'll probably never forget it. Your generation will be the first in America's history to live in an integrated world. You'll make your own mistakes, but they'll be different mistakes. Anyway son, what I'm saying to you is that Mr. Johnson is hurting. He was punished from birth for no good reason. He can't help but look at Ogie and see all the people that tried to deny him what he's earned just because he was black. He's protecting his daughter. You'll understand that instinct someday. There's nothing more powerful."

I thought for a moment and agreed with my father.

I had lunch with my father at the Chinese Sun House restaurant before he left for the airport. We talked about my little brother and all the famous people they were meeting. My parents were trying to nurture his career while still protecting his childhood. It was a difficult task and they were worried that they would fail him. My father said he wasn't worried about me because he was almost married by the time he was my age, but I knew I could never get married as young as him, even though I had offered the idea to Yonah's mother. I wasn't as mature as my father and didn't want to be. The world was forcing me to grow up, but there was nothing I wanted less. I was stumbling into a lot of things I didn't want to experience. I was enrolled to start college in the fall, but college wasn't an end to a means for me but simply a tool to avoid adulthood for a few more years. I had no idea what I wanted to do when I grew up because I didn't want to grow up. Life was picking me up and taking me for a ride I didn't want to be on and the more I tried to get off the faster it went.

Chapter 28

The four of us drove to the funeral together as the Society of Social Deviants. We hadn't mentioned the S.S.D., but that's what we were. It was our way to be one, to be united behind something bigger than us. And something bigger was what we needed because we felt small. As individuals, we were defeated and broken; but as the S.S.D. we were strong, we had possibilities.

The sun warmed the earth and our bodies at the graveyard as daffodils bloomed in the grassy edges of the cemetery that sat on a bluff above the Wahoo River. Thick yellow pollen covered the cars and coated the tombstones that marked lives of the past. Even the family limousine and hearse that had been washed that morning had a light coating of the yellow dust that was bringing a rebirth of life to the South.

I stepped carefully through the manicured lawn trying to avoid graves like landmines. Darwin, Ogie and Cassady followed so quietly I turned several times to see if they were still with me. A crowd gathered behind the green family tent with the name of the funeral home printed on the top. I wondered if this was to help families identify the correct place to go or simply advertising. The tent wasn't needed as a large magnolia tree covered the gravesite.

We stood with Darwin in the back, far from Elena's family, who sat in the front. I thought he should be with the family because he was the only man to ever love her like a woman and he was the closest thing to a marriage she would ever know. Their love was a love forever lasting, one that would never end because it was frozen by death.

The preacher started talking, but I didn't hear him as my mind wandered, creating a dreamlike and choppy service. One moment, I watched a bird flutter from the magnolia tree and the next, I watched a silver Mercedes pull up and two girls get out of the back. It was Kendi and Yonah. They were late, maybe on purpose. The driver, probably Kendi's mother, stayed in the car. The girls joined us at the back of the crowd and Ogie smiled at Kendi and she back and him, but they didn't hold hands or stand close as they might have the day before. After a few minutes, Kendi cried, but Yonah remained stoic. A breeze blew through the magnolia tree and shook the tent. I thought that this and everything else had worn down Yonah's soul and I felt guilty for everything that had happened around me and for not being able to protect the ones I loved. While I focused on getting drunk and laid, my friends fell to the hand of fate.

The preacher finished and a black lady in a gray dress began to sing. The words to Johnny Mercer's Moon River flowed from her lips with the grace and tone of Lena Horne. Ogie began to cry and Cassady reached over and hugged him. I looked to Darwin and saw a tear break from his eye and run down his face like a river making a new path. I held back my tears because I felt I didn't deserve the freedom of crying.

I saw Mother Elly at the edge of the cemetery. She looked right at me and I felt her strength. She had that look of a Southern woman that said volumes. She knew our hurt. I stopped listening to the song, but then something about Elly's expression gave me hope. I took a deep breath and straightened my back, refocusing on the words being sung for Elena. The time was coming, I could feel it. Evil would be defeated. I had no idea how, or when, but I knew.

Chapter 29

The service ended and the crowd returned to their cars with the quietness of mice in the night. A child had died and no one had an answer as to why. We walked back to my car and waited for the girls, but instead they returned to the Mercedes and drove away. We watched men from the funeral home lower the casket into the ground. Elena's mother screamed out and lurched toward the hole, but her husband caught her before she entered the grave.

Darwin looked to the sky and said something. I couldn't understand him, but I was sure he was cursing the heavens, cursing God. "I dreamed last night that it snowed on her grave, and when the snow melted, flowers grew in the soil that covered her body. The flowers created life and brought her back to us." Darwin began to sob. "This will never happen, though. She's gone forever." With Darwin's words I heard the first rumble of thunder from the west.

"We should go now. A storm is coming," Cassady said.

"I don't care. I don't care if I get hit by lighting and die," Darwin said between crying gasps.

"I care Darwin. I care if you die. We care. We need you," Ogie said as he tried to hug Darwin, but was pushed away when

Darwin stepped away from my car and fell to the ground in a sitting position.

Darwin put his face into his hands and cried so deeply that water ran through his fingers and dotted the ground below him. I knew Elena's death would change him, but until that moment I didn't know how much. Seeing him broken broke me and I began to cry. I had tried to be strong for Darwin, and then for Ogie, but the world I had known was over, the friends I had known were gone. How could this ever be made right? The confidence I'd briefly felt crumbled and I cried, even though I felt I didn't deserve to. But I did cry. Not for Elena, but for Darwin. Just as she had died, so had his youth. He would no longer be the boy I had known and loved. Now he was something different. Not yet a man, not a boy, and nothing in between I could recognize. She was gone and so was a part of him. Neither could ever be retrieved.

Drops of rain began to fall around us, but I felt none. Wind blew the trees and waves grew on the river, creating white caps, but I only noticed in the same way you notice background noises when dreaming. Cassady and Ogie picked Darwin up from the ground and placed him in the passenger seat of my car. I crawled into the back seat when Ogie suggested he drive. Darwin's Black Crowes tape we had been listening to before the storm was still in my car and he smiled when Ogie pushed it into the cassette player and heard a song we all liked. Tear after tear rolled down Darwin's face as he mouthed the words to "She Talks to Angels."

We drove out of the cemetery as the song played. I knew Darwin was thinking of her. I knew he would never be the same. I would never be able to hear that song again without thinking of her…and him.

Chapter 30

Music and wine calmed our souls after the funeral. There was no one to meet and nowhere to go, so we drove the back roads of Caswell County looking for places we had never been. There were few. Ogie drank little that night and drove my Mustang fast through the darkness. Our mood was somber, as would be expected, and there was little to say. Elena's dog, Misty, was in the back seat between Cassady and me. Her head rested on my lap as I stroked the soft red fur on the back of her neck. We were solemn and so was the dog. Misty missed the one she loved, her human mother. I didn't know how she knew Elena was gone, but she did.

We neared the Old Corinth Road Bridge when Darwin lit a joint and said, "Look at that car against that tree. Wonder if anyone needs help?"

I was surprised and distracted by the smell of the pot and didn't notice the car until Ogie slowed down and pointed the headlights toward the side of the road. The car's lights were dimming, indicating the car had been there long enough to drain the battery. Ogie stopped my car quickly and jumped out. Darwin followed while Cassady and I stayed in the backseat watching. Misty stood up and slipped from the car following Darwin.

"Hello, you okay?" Ogie yelled at the car. "You okay?"

"What," a man yelled back from the car. "Yes. I think I am. I just had a little accident," the man said before standing up from the car seat and then falling to the ground. "Well, would you look at that. I may be a little drunk." The driver giggled and wiped drool from his chin. "Would you fine gentlemen mind giving me a ride back to town?"

Ogie turned to us and laughed. "I think he's okay. Let's give him a ride," Ogie said as he helped the man to his feet.

Cassady and I agreed and climbed out the backseat of the Mustang so we could help, or maybe to get a better look at the drunken idiot. My laughter turned to fog in the cool night when I laughed as the man tried to stand before falling again. His clothes were covered in red mud from the mess he had created trying in a futile attempt to back out of the wet grass and away from the tree he had hit.

"Let's go help him," Cassady said before slipping in the mud.

"Watch out buddy. You don't want to end up like our drunk friend over there."

"Damn! I'm covered in mud," Cassady said. "This is a great way to end a shitty day."

"Don't worry about it. My car's about to get a lot dirtier when that guy gets in…and you back in."

I helped Cassady up and started to laugh, but stopped when I recognized the driver. It was the lawyer that had attacked Yonah— Taft E. Gregory. Frigid hate climbed my spine and I remained where I was for a moment trying to decide how to react. I knew I had to confront him. Now was the time. I just didn't know how. It didn't matter how, I decided, he had to be confronted.

The lawyer had haunted my dreams and changed the life of a dear friend. He had bended and twisted the laws to profit from the weak. After failing with the probate judge, I had spent countless hours thinking about ways to destroy him. I sought relief in visions of him hanging by the neck from a town oak tree or humiliating him in public, but those had only been thoughts. Thoughts I knew couldn't come true despite the rage he had released in me. I was young and powerless and he was protected by a system that had been growing stronger for well over a century. I believed I had no recourse. Until now.

I whispered to Cassady, "That's the man. That's the asshole that beat up and raped Yonah. That's Taft Gregory."

Cassady had been smiling after his fall in the mud, but his face changed like I had clicked a television remote. "Then let's kill that son of a bitch."

I believed he meant it, so I responded, "Cassady. We can't do that."

"Then what? What do we do? We're the S.S.D. We have to do something."

"S.S.D? What? I do want to kill him. I hate him with every part of my soul, but the S.S.D. has nothing to do with it," I said.

"It has everything to do with it. We're friends. We're brothers. It may be just a name, but it unites us. We stand up for each other and those that can't help themselves. This is one of those times," Cassady said speaking quietly.

"What are you two saying?" Darwin yelled over his shoulder at us before looking at Misty who was starting to growl at Gregory. "Quiet, girl. It's okay."

"I'll tell you what we're saying," Cassady said as he walked toward Darwin, Ogie and the lawyer. "That's the man that raped Yonah. That's the son of a bitch that beat her face black and blue. I say we do the same to him."

"What? Is this true?" Ogie asked us while looking at the Taft. "Are you the animal that hurt her? Are you Taft?"

"Yes, yes, I'm Taft. But, well boys it just wasn't like that. She was asking for it. She made it too easy. You guys know what it's like." Taft winked while reaching out to shake Ogie's hand.

Ogie slapped his hand away and then punched Taft with his left fist. Taft fell back into the mud again with a dull thwack.

Rain began to pour as we all stood staring.

When Taft tried to get up again, Ogie yelled, "You better stay down until we decide what to do with you.".

"Do with me? What do you mean?" Taft's face grew desperate and afraid. "Boys, men I should say. That was just one of those things. She was too easy. She wanted it. If you guys don't understand, then who will? I mean, you like to get laid don't you?"

"You sorry excuse for a human being," I screamed as I rushed to Gregory and kicked him in the ribs. Gregory folded over into fetal position and coughed and wheezed. "That wasn't getting laid. That was rape. You're an animal. You attacked someone weaker than you, someone that needed you to protect her. The county, her family, everyone trusted you and this is how you returned that trust. You're worth nothing. You are the lowest human being I've ever met. In fact, you're not even human." The words came easy because I had said them in my head dozens of times by then.

Gregory pushed himself back up to a seated position and held his arm over his stomach where I had kicked him. He looked at me and said, "You're the brother of that musician kid aren't you? Hey, I love his music. I have his tape in my car. Want to see it?" Gregory was used to getting his way with charm, but he was far beyond that with me.

"What? What are you talking about, you drunk idiot?" I turned to my friends. "So, what are we gonna do with him? We can't let him go."

"Yeah, what are we going to do?" Darwin asked reaching down to grab Misty's collar to keep her away from the lawyer.

"We can call the police and let him get a DUI," Ogie suggested.

"And then we'll go to jail for drinking underage. And how about the organic matter Darwin was smoking in my car? That's not going to fly with the cops," I said.

"Yeah, I agree," Darwin said. Misty pulled hard and Darwin struggled to stand in the mud. The dog sensed the evil in Gregory and wanted to destroy it.

Taft looked up at us while we deliberated. He smiled at us, but Misty showed her teeth and growled at the predator, causing the lawyer to cover his face and look away.

"I think we should kill him. We can't touch him with the law as long as he's protected by judges, but we can execute him." Cassady stepped next to Taft making the lawyer cower into himself.

"We can't kill him, Cassady," Darwin said putting his arm out to keep Cassady from getting closer to our prisoner.

"Why not?" Ogie asked. "Yonah is our friend. What if he did this to Elena?"

"That's right boys. You can't kill me. That's against the law. And you need to understand—" Gregory's words slurred as he became either drunker or more afraid, I couldn't tell which. "—under... understand that the crime scene people are very good at their jobs. They'll find out if you kill me."

"Somebody shut him up," I said before leaning over to the ground to pick up a tire iron Gregory had tried to use to dig his car out of the mud. "If you say another word I'm going to break your leg." I wasn't sure if I meant it or not.

"Okay, okay. Let's all just cool down," Gregory said reaching for his car door. "Y'all can go home. I'll find another way home and we can all talk this through on Monday."

Misty growled again when Gregory pulled himself from the ground using his car door. He was now standing and more intimidating than I expected. He stumbled and sat down in the driver's seat. "Let me give you my card and you can set something up with my secretary." The lawyer reached over to his passenger seat and moved quickly back to us. This time, he was holding a revolver. I could see in his eyes he meant to use it, but he didn't have a chance to cock it or even point it toward us before Misty jumped and clamped down on this wrist with her powerful jaws. She shook his arm like she was killing an opossum and forced Gregory to drop the gun into the mud. With his other hand, he beat on her back. His third blow caused her to yelp and fall to the ground next to the gun. I don't remember reacting, but I do remember the tire iron hitting his knee. Bone burst through his flesh and his khaki pants. His screams gave me some kind of satisfaction as the blood soaked his pants and squirted like water from a hose on a concrete driveway.

"Oh, my God!" He screamed like a wild pig. "Look what you did! Look what you did! You broke my fucking leg! You stupid kid! You broke my fucking leg!"

Cassady calmly picked Misty up and brought her back to the car. She was awake, whimpering and didn't seem to be hurt as badly as I had thought. "I can't believe we just did this," Cassady said as he carried the dog.

"What are you going to do now?" Gregory was crying. "What are you going to do with me? This is enough. You have revenge.

You have justice. I'll resign on Monday. I promise," Gregory pleaded.

"I don't believe you," Darwin said. "I simply don't believe you. My dad taught me how to spot a liar and you're a liar. You'll screw us over the first chance you get. I have no doubt we'll all end up in jail for this and then you'll sue our parents to top it off."

"Then what can we do?" asked Ogie.

Darwin said, "I don't know. I have to think."

Darwin walked back to my car and sat in the seat next to where Cassady had laid Misty. The dog crawled partly into his lap and licked his face. Her protection-driven anger had dissipated. Maybe she understood the physical threat from Gregory was gone or maybe she was too hurt to fight any more. Darwin took the bottle of wine from the floorboard of the car and sat in the seat and drank for at least five minutes while the rest of us switched from watching him to the lawyer. Every time the lawyer would start to talk or cry, one of us would look at him as a reminder to remain silent. Darwin finally stood up and returned to the group. He was carrying the bottle of wine in his right hand when he put his foot on the lawyer's leg and pushed the man from his car seat into the mud. The pain caused the lawyer to scream and then to pass out.

Darwin stood over Gregory until he regained consciousness. Then he looked at Ogie and spoke. "I have been thinking about what you said. About what I'd do if he did this to Elena and I know what I'd do if it were her. I'd execute him."

We didn't have time to absorb his proclamation, but the lawyer did and started to plead for his life. "I'm sorry. I'm so sorry. I was wrong. I'm a drunk. I hate myself. I don't know why I did what I did, what I do. I want to change. I'll change, I swear!"

Darwin responded with, "God might have mercy on you, but I won't." Then he raised the bottle high and brought it down with the force of a hammer against the head of Taft. The lawyer bounced to the ground like a ball and his head rose one more time before Darwin hit him again, and then again, and again.

None of us tried to stop Darwin as the blows broke the bones in Taft's face and pushed the back of his head into the mud. Taft was unconscious by the second blow and probably dead after the third or fourth blow, but Darwin hit him at least ten more times before stopping and falling back into the mud. Red blood mixed with white skull fragments and pink flesh in the wet, red Georgia clay. Killing was so simple.

"We did it. We just killed someone," I said, stepping back and feeling like I was seeing the event from outside my body. The rain stopped.

"We didn't kill anyone. Darwin did," Ogie said with fear in his eyes.

"No, we all did it," Cassady responded looking directly at Ogie. "We all did it because we are one."

"Okay, then. We all did." I was surprised that Ogie agreed so quickly, but then realized he would never have the same bond with anyone else that he had with us. None of us would.

"We'll figure out something," Darwin said. " I'm sorry y'all. I just thought about Elena and I saw her in that casket. I remembered how Yonah changed and it all just came together. I sorta snapped, but at the same time I felt more in control than ever before. I felt like it was my purpose to kill him." Darwin looked at the bottle in his hand. "I don't care. I don't care that I killed him. He deserved it."

"He did deserve it, Darwin. You did the right thing," Cassady said. "It was the only thing we could do. The law wasn't going to do anything. They can't and won't because it's so corrupt here. That bastard deserved it if anyone ever did. He hurt people we love and we hurt him. That's how karma works."

"Well, if this is karma, we're fucked because we just fucked up our own karma," Ogie said.

"I don't know about that," Cassady said turning to Ogie. "Maybe we're just doing karma's job. We just helped karma clean up evil."

I took the large duffle bag from the trunk of my car. It was the bag that Ogie's dad had used in Vietnam and I had borrowed and forgot to return a few weeks before. The bag was large, but fitting the body into the green canvas duffle bag was still difficult and took us all pushing and shoving. It started to rain again and the water and blood made the body slippery, but we were able to fold the body in half and finally get it into the bag. The clips were useless so Ogie used a piece of wire from the side of the road and tied the bag shut. We took the wine bottle with us and threw it out the window on our way to Gethsemane Gardens, miles from the crime scene.

The rain stopped again by the time we reached the Gardens, where Ogie pulled my car into the bushes so anyone driving down the road that night wouldn't see it. Even if they did, it was one of our regular haunts and no one would think twice about it. We each took turns carrying and dragging the bagged body through the woods toward the swamp. When we reached the fog covered waters, I weaved a heavy chain I kept in my car trunk through and around the bag. Ogie then lifted the canvas casket over his head and carried it a hundred feet from the shore—so far that no one would ever find Taft E. Gregory. With a splash, the most evil man I had ever known was left to lie with the snakes.

Chapter 31

College Street was quiet and asleep when we approached my house well after midnight. I was relieved when I didn't see police at my house and when no messages were on my answering machine.

The longest day of our lives was finally over, a day when we had buried a friend and killed a man. I was ready for it to end. Darwin picked up one of my little brother's guitars and strummed the cords to "She Talks to Angels." He hummed the words and we felt them.

"It's past midnight," Cassady said looking at my great-grandfather's clock on the mantel above the fireplace. "It's April Fool's Day. Do y'all want to go and get into some trouble?" He asked seriously, but I was sure he was joking.

"That's the last thing we need to do, Cass," Ogie said.

"Then what? What do we do next?"

Ogie seemed to think about his words before responding. "I don't know, but something will happen I'm sure. Something always happens next."

"That's right. Because we're the Society of Social Deviants," I noted.

Darwin stopped playing and looked at all of us. "I don't feel deviant any more. I feel old. I'm going home."

The lawyer was never found. His car was located the next day, but the rain washed away all the blood, so foul play was never suspected, especially when it was learned soon after that he had been embezzling money from his wards. It was assumed he had run off with the money to another country and ditched his car. Yonah wasn't the only one he had hurt and another family with more resources was able to uncover his actions with the help of a private investigator. Too bad they didn't catch him sooner, before he hurt her.

Judge Rush denied all wrongdoing and was quoted in the newspaper as saying, "No one ever came to me. I would have gladly investigated him and stopped him if anyone had simply come to me." A few months later, I heard he had a stroke and spent the last year of his life in a wheelchair sitting on his front porch whispering the word "witch" all day long and drooling on his bib. Rumor was that Mother Elly put a Hoodoo hex on him. While I don't think she was responsible for his stroke, I do think she made him believe it. She was right about one thing—evil always gets it in the end one way or another.

Two months after Gregory disappeared, we graduated from high school. It was a somber affair with a tribute to Elena, and though we were all sad to say goodbye, I think we were all relieved to get out of there and away from all the hurt.

Yonah received a full scholarship and went to college, despite her school funds being stolen. It took her two years of legal fighting to get her money back from the County. I saw her a few years later at our high school's homecoming football game. She was with her fiancé. Her eyes told me genuinely that she was glad to see me, but they also showed fear. Fear that I would reveal to her fiancé what had happened, but her fear was without merit. In the embrace of a handshake, I knew Yonah had found a knight to protect her through life. I could want nothing but good for her; she deserves it. I no longer live in River Falls. I left for college and now rarely return. Even then, it is most often a drive through as the pain still lingers. I grew older and changed, as the lucky do, but the memory of my hometown haunts me like a dead relative with unfinished business. I rarely see the boys of the S.S.D. as the act that drew us so close together that night now pushes us apart to each suffer separately. We agreed to never mention it again and to never reveal it to anyone. We even agreed to never tell our wives when we were married. We have buried the event so deeply, it's as if it never happened, but we have only to look in one another's eyes to know how real it still is.

Darwin became a lawyer doing pro bono work for the poor. He's continued to protect those that can't protect themselves. He won a large lawsuit a few years ago against a company that was dumping waste into the ground and poisoning a rural Louisiana town. He gave all but a modest salary to the families in the town.

Ogie married a debutante from Savannah and built a home at the edge of his family property. It sits on the same spot that once held a slave cabin. In some ironic way, I think it reminds him what his family did to others once and how far they came to accept a love that wasn't meant to be.

Cassady joined the Peace Corps and then became a Registered Nurse. When I do talk to him, I can hear pain in his voice. I think he's spent his entire adulthood making up for the sins of our past.

None of us know what happened to Kendi after she went to college. Her father died unexpectedly and the rest of her family moved away. The divide between black and white never shifted for them, but it did for us and that has to be enough.

When I talk about my teenage years, I tell people I was just an average kid in an average town. It was rather boring, I say. I can only wish it had really been that way.

CPSIA information can be obtained at www.ICGtesting.com
Printed in the USA
LVOW061337180512

282294LV00003B/2/P